Half-Baked Gourmet

PARTLY HOMEMADE TOTALLY DELICIOUS

FAMILY SUPPERS

200 Quick-and-Easy Meals • *Mary Jane Henderson*

A ROUNDTABLE PRESS BOOK

HPBOOKS

HPBooks
Published by The Berkley Publishing Group
A division of Penguin Group (USA) Inc.
375 Hudson Street
New York, New York 10014

www.roundtablepressinc.com
For Roundtable Press, Inc.:
Directors: Julie Merberg, Marsha Melnick
Executive Editor: Patty Brown
Editor: Sara Newberry

First edition: February 2005

This book has been cataloged with the Library of Congress.
ISBN 1-55788-435-8
Printed and bound in China

10 9 8 7 6 5 4 3 2 1

For Margot and Darren

ACKNOWLEDGMENTS

Sincere thanks to Sara Newberry, Patty Brown, Marsha Melnick, and Charles Kreloff for this delightful presentation of my recipes.

I would like to thank Mary Meyer for giving me a foundation from which to write this book. It is because of you that I know everything I know. Alison and Michael Betz, I am extremely grateful for your support—for all your tasting, chopping, and dishwashing, and all of the donated laundry soap.

To Lori Lynn, Jean, Princess Di, Tanya, Susan J, Pammie, Deborah, my friends at the G mag and MSL—my deepest appreciation for keeping me afloat in one way or another through many years of growth.

Thanks to Paula and Debbie, my role models for this undertaking, and to Hal, for being there at the right time. To Chris, I am indebted to you for keeping me at the gym at least once a week. And to Juana, "Gracias, mi hermana!"

And most of all to Jeff—because of you everything is possible.

Contents

For those who love to cook, meal preparation can be relaxing and creative. For those of us who don't, it can be a real drag. Nowadays we're busier than ever, and time with our family is more important than ever. No matter how experienced a cook you are, some nights it seems almost impossible to get dinner on the table. But with a little organization and a well-stocked pantry, great meals can be a snap. In **The Half-Baked Gourmet: Family Suppers,** I'll show you lots of ways to make family suppers easy.

GET READY FOR MONDAY

Sunday dinner can be a real treat, especially for the cook: Sunday is the perfect day to make a roast. Roasts don't need much attention until it's time to make gravy, and products such as sauce mixes and packaged broths make that easy. You can go on about your business while it cooks.

Buy a roast that's bigger than what you need, and after everyone enjoys Sunday's delicious meal, slice up leftovers and gently microwave them (always on medium power to avoid overcooking) or simmer them in gravy and make a fresh side dish and a salad (or reheat leftover potatoes and vegetables), and you've got a fast supper on Monday or Tuesday.

THINK QUICK

Oven or pan-roasting at high heat results in nicely seared meats and chicken with crispy skin. Be attentive to make sure the dish doesn't burn, and you'll have a wonderful dinner ready in half an hour.

THE FREEZER IS YOUR FRIEND

When you can, make foods ahead that you can freeze, such as soups, stews, and casseroles. Or when you're preparing one of these items for a night's meal, make a double batch—half for now, half for later. Thaw containers of soup or stew overnight in the refrigerator for easy reheating. you have a lot of meat left over after making a roast, freeze some of it as soon as possible plain or with gravy in portions of any size. Wrap meats for use in future casseroles in cup measures. Be sure to label and date everything you freeze.

TAKE STOCK

For busy week nights, plan ahead when shopping for the pantry and for fresh foods. If you keep a variety of ingredients on hand, cooking (and eating) will be fun. It's also a good idea to "mix it up" during the week. Serve a variety of dishes including lighter fare like salads and sandwiches, as well as meats, fish, and poultry. Serve eggs or pancakes occasionally—breakfast for dinner is an unexpected treat that your family will love.

WHAT'S YOUR BEEF?

Choosing the right cut of meat can be daunting, but there are basically three categories to remember: quick cooking, braising, and roasting.

For quick-cooking beef, look for steaks. Sirloin, filet mignon, and round are desirable choices. Sirloins or shell steaks are available boneless and can be cut into thick ($1/2$ inch) slices after grilling, broiling, or pan-frying. Flank steaks, London broil, and top and bottom round can be cooked in the same manner, but they must be more thinly sliced—about ⅛ inch thick—for serving because of their low fat content. Otherwise the meat will be unpleasantly tough to chew.

For braising, choose the brisket and less expensive cuts, such as the rump and chuck. They require slow gentle simmering to reach the point of being tender. Brisket is perfect for slicing or shredding after braising.

The king of all roasts is the prime rib. It is available boneless or semi-boneless. The boneless filet can be cooked either in individual steaks or as a roast.

Many supermarkets sell select and/or choice cuts of meat; specialty butchers often sell prime cuts, which are much more expensive. Historically, marbling—or fat content—is the determining factor for grading, and it was thought that marbling equaled tenderness, but tenderness is actually a genetic trait. If you don't see a label that says USDA choice on the package, the meat is probably "select." If given the option, buy choice, because chances are you will get a superior product, but there is nothing wrong with select.

SUPER SHOPPER

Look for specials on meats and poultry in the supermarket circular and stock up. Typically, my market has seasonal specials with the customer in mind. I look for meat and poultry products that are all natural without additives—Murray's and Bell and Evans are two brands that I prefer.

I also like to buy in bulk from my local Costco; I use a kitchen scale to help divide up the portions, and freeze meat and poultry for later use. For best results, wrap meat or chicken in freezer paper, label clearly (be sure to include the date), and freeze ASAP for up to three months. Be sure to rotate your supply: place newer purchases behind what you already have. The night before cooking, place the package on a plate and transfer to the refrigerator. If the meat is still slightly frozen when you're ready to cook, you can quickly thaw it in the microwave. It's best to microwave meats unwrapped, on a plate, at 30 percent power, so you don't cook them instead of thawing. Cover with a paper towel before zapping, and be sure to rotate and turn the meat over during the process for even thawing.

VEG-A-MATIC

Keep lots of frozen vegetables on hand for using in recipes and for simple, no-fuss side dishes. I like Green Giant brand vegetables without sauce in the boiling bags because they have a long freezer life, but Birds Eye brand vegetables are also of good quality. I especially like their French-cut green beans and baby peas. My local supermarket sells a great variety of different frozen vegetables from diced butternut squash to pearl onions. Many of their vegetables are sold in one-pound bags, which are more reasonably priced.

Whichever brand you choose, frozen vegetables are superior to canned and a great way to insure that you and your family get your veggies. For simple vegetable side dishes, cook veggies according to package directions. To quickly thaw vegetables to add to recipes, place in a colander and run cold water over them, thaw gently in the microwave at 30% power, or thaw overnight in the refrigerator.

DAIRY DOGMA

I like to buy vacuum-sealed hunks of imported cheeses from the cheese section for dicing and slicing, and use them up quickly once the package is opened. For convenience, keep packaged shredded cheeses in sealable plastic bags in the freezer for up to two months. Be sure to squeeze all of the air out of the bag before resealing.

Make it a rule to have a pound or two of butter in the freezer and two dozen eggs in the refrigerator. Most baking recipes call for large eggs, so that's a good standard size to keep on hand, and unsalted butter is better for baking.

Aside from milk and heavy cream, it's a good idea to keep sour cream, cream cheese, and ricotta cheese on hand. These have a relatively long shelf life and can be counted on to add tang and creaminess to many dishes—not just to the familiar baked potatoes and toast. I use reduced-fat sour cream and cream cheese, because I can save on calories without missing out on texture. Nonfat products tend to lack flavor and the creamy texture, so I don't recommend them. Cream cheese and sour cream can both be used to make creamy sauces without the addition of another ingredient.

I prefer whole-milk fresh ricotta cheese that I buy at a specialty market; its creamy texture blows away the supermarket brands, but it doesn't keep for very long.

BIGGER THAN A BREAD BOX

Keep a supply of various breads, fresh tortillas (both corn and flour), and pizza dough on hand in the freezer. Many supermarkets sell balls of dough in the refrigerator section near the cheese, and some sell it frozen, but for the best pizza dough, become friendly with the owner of your neighborhood pizzeria and buy dough there,

Self-rising flour and cornmeal mix are great for quick biscuits, muffins, and savory potpies and cobblers. Many brands of cornmeal mix have shortening already added—Hodgson Mills doesn't, and I prefer it for that reason. Martha White self-rising cornmeal is another great product.

PANTRY PROUD

Pick up jarred, bottled, and canned goods to keep on hand, such as beans, sauces, jams, marinades, condiments, dressings, and broth. I prefer Swanson's low-sodium chicken broth because it tastes most like homemade. I only use Hellmann's mayonnaise (but I like both the regular and the reduced-fat varieties), and I usually buy either Hero imported Swiss preserves or St. Dalfour 100% fruit spreads. I like to make my own salad dressing, but usually have a couple of bottles of prepared dressings made with all-natural ingredients, like Newman's Own, and preferably without added sugar, like Annie's Organics.

For more exotic flavors, I like Taste of Thai Red Curry Base—it helps you whip up an exotic Thai dish in minutes that would take two or three times the time and ingredients if made from scratch. Patak sauces and marinades do basically the same for Indian dishes. When buying sauces and marinades, be aware that many of them contain large amounts of sodium, so you'll want to watch how much salt you add to a dish that contains these.

Keep a supply of sauce mixes and other flavoring packets such as McCormick's taco seasoning and Serv-a-gravy sauce mix—they come in handy and will keep their flavor for about a year.

Dried herbs and spices are also useful to keep on hand. Store jars of dried herbs and spices at room temperature (not above the stove), and they'll keep their flavor for about a year. A test for a dried herb or spice's potency is to take a whiff when you open the jar. if there's no aroma, chances are there's no flavor either.

A product that I love to use is Jane's Krazy Mixed-Up Salt. Unlike other seasoned salts, it is made with coarse salt, instead of fine salt, which makes it easier to control. I prefer its taste to that of other brands I've tried. Look for it in your supermarket's spice aisle or order it online. When I refer to seasoned salt in the recipes in this book, I'm talking about Jane's.

For salt-free seasoning, I use Mrs. Dash Original Blend. There are other blends available, such as garlic and herb and minced onion blend. Use whichever one you like best.

GET FRESH—IT'S IN THE BAG!

Many supermarkets now sell house-brand bagged cut-up fresh vegetables, cello-wrapped lettuces, and packaged sliced exotic mushrooms that tend to be less expensive than national brands.

Some of the most exciting new products available are ready-to-cook frozen potatoes. Look for Fresh From the Start diced potatoes or Cascadian Farm shredded potatoes, which are blanched or frozen without additives. Potatoes that are treated with additives have an unpleasant aftertaste, even after repeated rinsing. Look for instant potatoes that are pure potato, such as Betty Crocker Potato Buds, for the best results in soups and shepherd's pies.

EQUIPMENT

Always use an internal meat thermometer when preparing a roast. Instant-read thermometers are great for smaller roasts, but use an ovenproof thermometer for a rib roast, fresh ham, or leg of lamb.

Cutting boards are available in wood, hardened rubber, and glass. Glass cutting boards are very hard on knife blades—I don't recommend them. I prefer wooden boards, but they require more care and upkeep than hardened rubber boards. Whichever cutting board you choose, be sure to wash and dry it thoroughly after every use, and never cut cooked items on a cutting board that you have just used for raw items. I also keep a couple of different sizes on hand. And if you don't have a cutting board with grooves, it's a great idea to invest in one to catch the delicious meat juices every time you make a roast.

FREEZER, FRIDGE AND PANTRY SHELF

Next time you're at your supermarket, check out some of the items I've used for the recipes in this book. They'll help you save time and have fun in the kitchen while you're preparing wholesome meals for your family and friends. All that's missing are the occasional fresh items, such as fruits, vegetables, meats, and herbs.

IN THE FREEZER…

PASTRY/BREAD
Pillsbury prepared pie crusts
Pizza/bread dough
10-inch flour tortillas
Corn tortillas
6-inch egg-roll wrappers
Italian bread
Marble rye
Sub rolls
Hamburger buns
Hard rolls

VEGETABLES
Chopped onion
Bell pepper stir-fry (with onion)
Baby (Le Sueur®) peas
Baby carrots
Crinkle-cut carrots
Cut green beans
French-cut green beans
White or yellow corn
Chopped spinach
Leaf spinach
Chopped collards
Brussels sprouts
Okra
Black-eyed peas
Artichokes
Pearl onions
Cascadian Farm® organic frozen
    hash browns
Alexia® oven fries (with olive oil
    and sea salt)
Frozen diced butternut squash
Frozen sliced zucchini

CURED AND SMOKED MEATS
Oscar Mayer® ready-to-serve
    bacon
Hormel® ready-to-serve bacon
Hormel® real crumbled bacon
Baked or boiled ham
Sliced turkey pepperoni
Sliced prosciutto
Thick-sliced smoked bacon
Frozen Philly-style sandwich
    steaks
Jimmy Dean's® fully-cooked
    sausages
Hot dogs
Bratwurst
Smoked pork chops
Kielbasa

NUTS AND DRIED FRUIT
Sliced almonds
Pecans
Walnuts
Salted roasted cashews
Dry roasted peanuts
Dried cranberries
Raisins
Currants
Dried mixed fruit

IN THE FRIDGE…

DAIRY
Large eggs
Unsalted butter
Lightly salted butter
Milk
Buttermilk
Heavy cream
Half-and-half
Sour cream
Stonyfield® plain whole-milk
    yogurt
Ricotta cheese
Kraft® Philadelphia® cream
    cheese
Polly-O® shredded mozzarella
    cheese
Shredded Mexican blend cheese
Shredded cheddar cheese
Shredded Monterey Jack
    cheese
Fresh goat cheese
Gruyère cheese
Grated Parmesan Cheese,
    (preferably Parmigiano
    Reggiano)
Kraft® Cracker Barrel®
    sandwich slices
Jarlsburg slices
Provolone slices
Imported Swiss cheese
Stella® crumbled Gorgonzola
Blue cheese crumbles
Feta cheese crumbles

CONDIMENTS AND SAUCES
Peeled garlic cloves
Minced garlic
Hellmann's® mayonnaise
Blue-cheese dressing
Smucker's® creamy natural
    peanut butter
Kikkoman® soy sauce

Kikkoman® stir-fry sauce
Kokkoman® teriyaki sauce
Thai fish sauce
Roland® satay barbecue sauce
French's® wasabi mayonnaise
French's® chipotle mayonnaise
Maille® Dijon mustard
Honey mustard
Whole-grain mustard
Heinz® ketchup
Barbecue sauce
Frank's® Red Hot® sauce
Gold's® horseradish
Lea and Perrins® worcestershire
    sauce
Green Mountain Gringo® salsa
Herdez® salsa verde
Buitoni® Alfredo sauce
Buitoni® pesto
Prepared guacamole

IN THE PANTRY

MIXES
Bread, Muffin, and Stuffing
Hodgson Mills® cornbread and
    muffin mix
Betty Crocker® Bisquick®
Martha White® self-rising
    cornmeal mix
Low-sodium stuffing mix
Dried herb-seasoned stuffing

Soup and Sauce
Knorr® onion soup mix
Knorr® leek soup mix
Knorr® roasted garlic soup mix

Serv-a-gravy® brown sauce mix
Knorr® roast-chicken gravy mix
Knorr® turkey gravy mix

PASTA, BREAD, AND GRAINS
Near East instant couscous
Pearl barley
Instant polenta
Fine egg noodles
Medium-size shells
Fusilli pasta
Spaghetti
Carolina® long-grain white rice
Instant brown rice
Instant white rice
Betty Crocker® Potato Buds®
Nabisco® Original Premium®
    saltine crackers
Bearitos® unsalted tortilla chips
Potato chips
6-inch corn tostadas
Wide chow mein noodles
Parmesan cheese straws

OILS AND VINEGARS
Extra-virgin olive oil
Red wine vinegar
Cider vinegar
Distilled white vinegar
Balsamic vinegar
Asian (dark) sesame oil
Hollywood® safflower oil

SAUCES AND SPREADS
(refrigerate after opening)
Rao's Homemade™ marinara
    sauce
Victoria® tomato-basil sauce
Victoria® porcini-tomato sauce
Victoria® arrabiata sauce
Roasted red pepper–tomato sauce
Patak's® creamy coconut sauce
Patak's® tandoori sauce (tikka
    masala)
Patak's® spicy ginger and garlic
    (tandoori) marinade
Patak's® sweet peppers and
    coconut sauce
Pizza sauce
Goya® sofrito
Goya® recaito
Goya® citrus marinade
Coleslaw dressing
Oak Hill Farms® Vidalia onion
    vinaigrette
Annie's Organic® salad
    dressings
Newman's Own® balsamic
    vinegar and oil dressing
Newman's Own® roasted garlic
    dressing
Newman's Own® Caesar
    dressing
Kraft® Velveeta®
Tomato paste
Pure maple syrup
Hero® peach preserves
Hero® orange marmalade
Candied ginger purée

VEGETABLES
(refrigerate after opening)

Contadina® canned crushed
   tomatoes in purée
Contadina® stewed tomatoes
   with garlic
Roasted red peppers with garlic
   in olive oil
Chipotle chiles in adobo
Chopped mild green chiles
Small artichoke hearts
Pitted green olives
Pitted kalamata olives
Niçoise olives
Sliced mushrooms
Straw mushrooms
Sliced water chestnuts
Bean sprouts
Flower-cut baby corn
Solid pack pumpkin
Green peppercorns in brine
Goya® cannellini beans
Goya® pinto beans
Goya® red beans
Goya® chickpeas
Old El Paso® low-fat refried
   beans
Claussen's® bread 'n' butter
   pickle slices

FRUIT
(refrigerate after opening)

Peaches in fruit juice
Pears in fruit juice
Mandarin oranges
Dole® pineapple chunks in juice

BROTHS
(refrigerate after opening)

Swanson® low-sodium chicken
   broth
Swanson® low-sodium beef
   broth
Atlantic® clam juice

SEAFOOD
(Refrigerate after opening)

Bumble Bee® crabmeat
Bumble Bee® tiny shrimp
Bumble Bee® solid white tuna
   in water
Progresso® tuna in olive oil

SPICE SHELF AND DRY GOODS

Molasses
Honey
Kosher salt
Jane's Krazy Mixed-Up® salt
Salt-free lemon pepper
Pepper
Cayenne
Caraway seeds
Cinnamon
Red pepper flakes
Dried thyme
Italian herbs
Rosemary
Oregano
Pumpkin pie spice
Ground cloves
Ground allspice
Ground cumin
Ground ginger
Sesame seeds

Dried tarragon
Turmeric
Mustard seeds
Ancho chili powder
Mrs. Dash®
A Taste of Thai® red curry base
Chef Paul's® Cajun Magic®
   seasoning blend
Sharwood's® tandoori spice
   blend
McCormick® taco seasoning
Hormel® crumbled bacon
Dried porcini mushrooms
Pam® original vegetable-oil
   cooking spray
Granulated sugar
Light brown sugar
Presto® self-rising flour
All-purpose flour
Granola
Plain dried breadcrumbs
Italian-style seasoned
   breadcrumbs
Sweet potatoes or yams
Baking potatoes
Yukon gold potatoes
Garlic
Yellow onions
Red onions

WINE AND LIQUOR

Dry sherry
Brandy
Dry red wine

Flash in the Pan

Chicken with Mushrooms and Artichokes

Roasted or steamed new potatoes would pair perfectly with this rich dish.

PREP TIME: 5 MINUTES • COOK TIME: 15 MINUTES • MAKES: 4 SERVINGS

1 tablespoon olive oil
4 skinless boneless chicken breast halves
   (6 ounces each)
1 packet (1.2 ounces) turkey gravy mix
½ teaspoon dried tarragon, crumbled
1 can (8 ounces) sliced mushrooms,
   drained
1 cup frozen artichokes, thawed and
   quartered

1. In a nonstick 12-inch skillet over medium-high heat, heat the oil. Add chicken and cook, turning once, until browned, about 4 minutes.

2. Meanwhile, in a medium bowl, whisk together gravy mix, tarragon, and 1½ cups water. Transfer chicken to a plate, add sauce to pan, and bring to boiling, whisking. Return chicken and any juices that have collected to the skillet. Reduce heat to medium-low and simmer, turning chicken occasionally, 5 minutes. Add mushrooms and artichokes and cook until chicken is just cooked through, about 5 minutes longer.

Heavenly Deviled Chicken Thighs

To make thighs on the bone, just cook 10 to 15 minutes longer. Serve with Creamed Spinach (p. 142) and any kind of potato.

PREP TIME: 1 HOUR • COOK TIME: 25 MINUTES • MAKES: 6 SERVINGS

Butter for greasing foil
2 cups buttermilk
1 tablespoon Dijon mustard
12 boneless chicken thighs (with or without skin)
1½ cups cubed herb-seasoned stuffing

1. Arrange oven rack to upper third of oven and heat oven to 425°F. Line a baking sheet with foil. Lightly butter the foil.

2. In a large bowl, combine buttermilk and mustard. Add chicken and let stand at room temperature 1 hour, or refrigerate for up to 8 hours.

3. In a food processor with the steel blade attached, pulse stuffing to make medium crumbs and place in a large sealable plastic bag. Add 4 pieces chicken, close bag completely, and shake to coat. Transfer to prepared baking sheet. Repeat with remaining chicken.

4. Roast chicken until golden and cooked through, 20 to 25 minutes. Let rest 5 minutes before serving.

Chicken Thighs with Thai Peanut Sauce

Serve with rice noodles (found in the Asian section of your supermarket), which can be a fun alternative to rice.

PREP TIME: 10 MINUTES • COOK TIME: 40 MINUTES • MAKES: 3 TO 6 SERVINGS

2 tablespoons vegetable oil
2 teaspoons jarred minced garlic
1/4 teaspoon salt
6 large chicken thighs
2/3 cup satay sauce
Unsalted dry-roasted peanuts, chopped, for garnish
Thinly sliced scallions, for garnish

1. Place oven rack in upper third of oven and heat oven to 450°F. Line a baking sheet with foil, then spray with vegetable oil cooking spray.

2. In a large bowl, whisk together oil, garlic, and salt. Add chicken, toss to coat, and arrange skin-side up on prepared baking sheet. Bake until juices run clear when a thigh is pierced with a fork, 30 to 40 minutes.

3. Pour satay sauce into a clean bowl. When chicken is cooked, turn hot pieces in sauce to coat. To serve, divide chicken among plates, spoon sauce over, and sprinkle with peanuts and scallions.

Fried Chicken with Cream Gravy

This dish is my favorite birthday dinner. The chicken is fried, but it doesn't absorb a lot of oil. Creamy Dreamy Mashed Potatoes (p. 155) are a must with this Southern-inspired specialty.

PREP TIME: 20 MINUTES • COOK TIME: 40 MINUTES • MAKES: 4 SERVINGS

1 chicken (3 to 3½ pounds), cut into eighths, wing tips discarded
½ cup plus ⅔ cup milk
½ teaspoon seasoned salt
Freshly ground black pepper
¾ cup plus 1½ tablespoons all-purpose flour
2 cups vegetable oil, for frying
⅓ cup low-sodium chicken broth

1. In a large bowl, combine chicken, ½ cup milk, seasoned salt, and ¼ teaspoon pepper. Let stand 5 minutes. Place wet chicken with ¾ cup flour in a large plastic bag; seal, shake, and let stand 10 minutes.

2. Heat oil in a deep 10-inch skillet (with a lid) over medium-high heat. Remove chicken from flour and carefully add all the pieces to the hot oil. Cover and cook 5 minutes. Turn and cook 5 minutes more, until chicken is golden on both sides. Using tongs, transfer chicken to a plate. Carefully discard oil (an old coffee can is perfect for this; just remember that the can will get very hot).

3. Heat oven to 200°F. Return chicken to skillet and add ½ cup water. Cover and cook over medium heat, turning, until chicken is crisp and just cooked through, about 25 minutes. Transfer to an ovenproof platter and place in oven to keep warm.

4. Discard all but about 2 tablespoons fat from skillet. Whisk in 1½ tablespoons flour and cook 1 minute. Gradually whisk in broth and ⅔ cup milk; bring to a boil over medium-high heat, whisking. Cook 3 minutes; season to taste with salt and pepper. Serve chicken on the warmed platter with gravy on the side.

Pesto Chicken

Pasta (linguine or fettuccine would be ideal) and an Herbed Tomato Salad (p. 163) will complete this meal nicely.

PREP TIME: 10 MINUTES • COOK TIME: 25 MINUTES • MAKES: 4 SERVINGS

¼ cup all-purpose flour
4 large skinless chicken thighs (7 ounces each)
1 tablespoon olive oil
½ cup jarred Alfredo sauce
2 tablespoons prepared basil pesto

1. In a large sealable plastic bag, combine flour and chicken pieces. Close bag, sealing completely, and shake to coat chicken. In a medium nonstick skillet over medium-high heat, heat oil.

2. Remove chicken pieces from bag and shake off excess flour. Add chicken to skillet, cook 2 minutes, turn, and cook until browned, about 2 minutes longer. Transfer chicken to a plate; discard fat from pan. Add Alfredo sauce, pesto, and 1 cup water; stir to blend. Return chicken to pan and bring to boiling. Reduce heat to medium, cover, and simmer, turning occasionally, until chicken is cooked through, about 20 minutes.

Bacon and Cheddar Chicken

Steamed broccoli and microwave-baked potatoes are the sides I like to have with this tasty chicken.

PREP TIME: 5 MINUTES • **COOK TIME: 15 MINUTES** • **MAKES: 4 SERVINGS**

1 tablespoon vegetable oil
4 large skinless boneless chicken breast
    halves (about 6 ounces each), trimmed
    of fat
⅓ cup crumbled bacon
½ cup frozen chopped onion
½ cup milk
6 ounces shelf-stable cheese, sliced

1. In a large nonstick skillet over medium-high heat, heat oil. Add chicken and cook, turning once, until golden on both sides and just cooked through, 7 to 8 minutes. Transfer chicken to a plate and cover with foil to keep warm.

2. Add bacon to skillet and cook, stirring, over medium heat until crisp, about 2 minutes. Add onion and cook, stirring, 3 minutes. Add milk and cheese and stir until smooth. Return chicken and any juices that have collected to pan and turn chicken in sauce to coat. To serve, transfer to plates and spoon sauce over.

Speedy Chicken Parmesan

A quick dusting of flour makes this the lightest Chicken Parm on earth. For variety, add sliced mushrooms or zucchini to the pan and sauté with a little butter before adding the broth and sauce. Spaghetti and a green salad with a bottled balsamic dressing will be perfect alongside.

PREP TIME: 10 MINUTES • COOK TIME: 20 MINUTES • MAKES: 4 SERVINGS

4 large skinless boneless chicken breast halves (about 6 ounces each), trimmed of fat

Salt and freshly ground black pepper

2 tablespoons all-purpose flour

2 tablespoons extra-virgin olive oil

¼ cup low-sodium chicken broth

1 cup tomato basil pasta sauce

2 cups (8 ounces) shredded mozzarella cheese

2 tablespoons chopped fresh parsley, for garnish

1. Season chicken with salt and pepper; sprinkle with flour.

2. In a large nonstick skillet over medium high heat, heat oil. Add chicken and cook, turning once, until nicely golden on both sides and just cooked through, 7 to 8 minutes. Transfer chicken to a plate and cover with foil to keep warm.

3. Add broth and pasta sauce to the pan and bring to boiling. Reduce heat to medium and simmer until liquid is reduced by half, about 5 minutes. Return chicken to pan, top with mozzarella, cover, and cook until cheese is melted, 1 to 2 minutes. Transfer each piece of chicken to a plate and spoon sauce around and over the chicken. Sprinkle with parsley and serve.

Chicken Stewed with Black Olives and Capers

Serve with crusty bread and 1-2-3 House Salad (p. 160).

PREP TIME: 10 MINUTES • COOK TIME: 40 MINUTES • MAKES: 4 SERVINGS

1 chicken (3½ pounds), cut into 8 pieces
¼ cup all-purpose flour
2 tablespoons extra-virgin olive oil
1 cup frozen chopped onion
1 can (28 ounces) stewed sliced tomatoes
   with garlic
¾ cup low-sodium chicken broth
⅓ pound pitted black olives, such as
   kalamata, rinsed
2 tablespoons capers in brine, drained
2 tablespoons finely chopped Italian
   parsley, for garnish

1. In a large bowl, combine the chicken pieces and flour. Toss until chicken is evenly coated.

2. In a large deep skillet over medium-high heat, heat oil. Add chicken to pan; cook, turning once or twice, until golden, about 6 minutes. Transfer pieces to a plate.

3. Discard fat from skillet. Reduce heat to medium-low, add onion, and cook, stirring, for 2 minutes. Stir in tomatoes, broth, and ¾ cup water. Return chicken to pan, increase heat to medium-high, and bring to boiling. Reduce heat to medium-low, cover, and simmer until chicken is cooked through, about 30 minutes.

4. To serve, transfer chicken to a deep serving dish, stir olives and capers into sauce, and spoon sauce over chicken. Sprinkle parsley on top.

Spinach and Goat Cheese Chicken Roulades

Serve these colorful roulades hot with a side of your favorite pasta.

PREP TIME: 20 MINUTES • COOK TIME: 15 MINUTES • MAKES: 4 SERVINGS

Butter for greasing dish
¼ cup (2 ounces) fresh goat cheese
¼ cup (2 ounces) cream cheese
1 package (9 ounces) frozen chopped
   spinach, thawed and squeezed dry
Salt and freshly ground black pepper
4 large, thin chicken cutlets (1½ pounds
   total)
1 tablespoon olive oil
1 cup porcini and portobello tomato sauce

1. Heat oven to 400°F. Butter a 9-inch-square glass baking dish and set aside.

2. In a small bowl, stir together goat cheese, cream cheese, spinach, and ¼ teaspoon each salt and pepper. Lay cutlets smooth-side down on a sheet of wax paper.

Divide spinach mixture evenly among cutlets, mounding in the center of each. Roll each cutlet around mixture and secure with toothpicks. Season each roll with salt and pepper.

3. In a 10-inch nonstick skillet over medium-high heat, heat oil. Add chicken rolls and cook, turning, until golden on all sides, about 4 minutes. Transfer to prepared baking dish.

4. In a small saucepan, warm sauce. Spoon over chicken and bake until chicken is just cooked through, 8 to 10 minutes. Transfer rolls to plates, remove toothpicks, spoon sauce over each roll, and serve immediately.

Margot's Favorite Chicken Fingers

Kids (of any age) will go crazy for these chicken fingers. They're great with just a squeeze of fresh lemon, or serve them with barbecue sauce, blue cheese dip, or honey mustard. Cut-up fresh vegetables that can also be dipped, such as celery sticks or baby carrots, will round out this fun meal.

PREP TIME: 25 MINUTES • COOK TIME: 15 MINUTES • MAKES: 4 SERVINGS

1¼ pounds chicken tenders
½ cup buttermilk
½ cup all-purpose flour
1 teaspoon dried thyme
1 teaspoon seasoned salt
1 cup vegetable oil
½ cup olive oil

1. In a medium bowl, combine chicken and buttermilk. Toss to coat and let stand 10 minutes.

2. In a sealable plastic bag, combine flour, thyme, and seasoned salt. Add chicken, seal, and shake well. Let stand 15 minutes.

3. In a large heavy skillet over medium heat, heat oils until they ripple. Using tongs, remove half of the chicken strips one at a time, shake off excess flour, and place in pan. Cook, turning occasionally, until golden and just cooked through, about 5 minutes. Use tongs to transfer to a paper towel–lined plate and repeat with remaining chicken. Serve immediately with your choice of dipping sauce.

Potato Chip Chicken Tenders

For a fun effect, use ruffled potato chips. Serve these yummy chicken tenders with Zippy Oven Fries (p. 157) and your favorite ketchup.

PREP TIME: 15 MINUTES • COOK TIME: 10 MINUTES • MAKES: 4 SERVINGS

5 heaping cups potato chips
$\frac{1}{2}$ cup all-purpose flour
3 large eggs
1 $\frac{1}{4}$ pounds chicken tenders
$\frac{1}{2}$ cup milk

1. Place chips in a sealable plastic bag, remove excess air, and close completely. Using a rolling pin, crush chips, then transfer them to a shallow bowl. Place flour and eggs separately in 2 more bowls. Lightly beat eggs with a fork.

2. Move oven rack to upper third of oven and heat oven to 450°F. Line a baking sheet with foil and spray with vegetable oil cooking spray.

3. Place chicken in the milk and toss to coat. Working with 1 piece of chicken at a time, roll in flour, dip in egg, roll in crushed potato chips, and transfer to prepared pan. Repeat with remaining ingredients.

4. Bake chicken tenders until golden and just cooked through, about 10 minutes.

Chicken Breasts with Mushrooms and Rosemary

Pan-frying can be the quickest way to a delicious meal. Serve with Nutty Herbed Rice Pilaf (p. 166) or any potato or pasta dish.

PREP TIME: 10 MINUTES • COOK TIME: 15 MINUTES • MAKES: 4 SERVINGS

4 large skinless boneless chicken breast
   halves (about 6 ounces each), trimmed
Salt and freshly ground black pepper
2 tablespoons all-purpose flour
2 tablespoons olive oil
2 teaspoons jarred minced garlic
1 package (8 ounces) sliced fresh
   mushrooms
1 cup low-sodium chicken broth
½ teaspoon dried rosemary, crumbled
1½ tablespoons unsalted butter

1. Season chicken with salt and pepper; sprinkle with flour.

2. In a large nonstick skillet over medium-high heat, heat oil. Cook chicken, turning once, until golden on both sides and just cooked through, 7 to 8 minutes. Transfer chicken to a plate and keep warm.

3. Add garlic and mushrooms to pan and cook, stirring, 2 minutes. Add broth and rosemary, bring to boiling and cook until reduced by half, about 2 minutes. Reduce heat to low, stir in butter, and season to taste. Turn chicken in sauce to coat, then transfer to plates. Spoon sauce over and serve immediately.

Happy Vegetable-Chicken Stir-Fry

Choose the most colorful vegetable blend you can find. Serve over rice or pasta.

PREP TIME: 5 MINUTES • COOK TIME: 10 MINUTES • MAKES: 4 SERVINGS

2 tablespoons vegetable oil
1¼ pounds skinless boneless chicken
   breasts, sliced crosswise into ¼-inch-
   thick slices
1 bag (1 pound) frozen stir-fry vegetables
3 tablespoons stir-fry sauce
1 bag (8 ounces) fresh bean sprouts
¼ cup orange juice

1. In a nonstick 12-inch skillet over medium-high heat, heat oil. Add chicken and stir-fry until just cooked through, 2 to 3 minutes. Transfer to a plate.

2. Add vegetables and stir-fry sauce to skillet and cook, stirring, until vegetables are tender and sauce is reduced to a glaze, about 4 minutes. Add bean sprouts and orange juice and cook until sprouts are heated though, 2 to 3 minutes. Return chicken to skillet and toss to mix. Serve immediately.

Pineapple Chicken

For a festive touch, sprinkle with sliced scallion greens and chopped roasted peanuts just before serving. Rice would be the ideal bed for this fruity dish.

PREP TIME: 5 MINUTES • **COOK TIME: 15 MINUTES** • **MAKES: 4 SERVINGS**

2 tablespoons teriyaki sauce

2 cans (8 ounces each) pineapple chunks in juice

4 large skinless boneless chicken breast halves (about 6 ounces each), trimmed of fat

⅔ cup low-sodium chicken broth

2 tablespoons butter

1. In a medium bowl, combine teriyaki sauce and ¼ cup juice from pineapple. Add chicken and turn to coat.

2. Heat a nonstick 12-inch skillet over medium-high heat and spray with vegetable oil cooking spray. Remove chicken from bowl and add, smooth-side down, to pan. Cook, turning once, until browned, 1 to 2 minutes per side. Add pineapple chunks, juice, and teriyaki mixture to skillet. Reduce heat to medium and bring to simmering. Cook, turning often, until just cooked through, 6 to 8 minutes.

3. Transfer chicken to plates. Stir butter into sauce and spoon sauce over chicken.

Honey-Lime Grilled Chicken

Buy already-quartered chickens the night before and leave them to marinate until you're ready to cook. Served with Golden Potato Salad with Green Chilis (p. 153), Herbed Tomato Salad (p. 163), or Seedy Slaw (p. 162), this is a perfect backyard party dish.

PREP TIME: 35 MINUTES • COOK TIME: 45 MINUTES • MAKES: 6 SERVINGS

¼ cup olive oil
¼ cup lime juice
1 teaspoon minced garlic
2 tablespoons honey mustard
2 chickens, quartered (3½ pounds each)
Salt and freshly ground black pepper

1. In a large bowl, whisk together the oil, lime juice, garlic, and honey mustard. Add chicken pieces, turning in marinade. Cover and chill 30 minutes or overnight.

2. Prepare grill. Season chicken with salt and pepper, arrange pieces on grill rack, cover, and cook over medium flame, turning, until crisp and just cooked through, about 45 minutes.

VARIATION

Honey-Lime Roasted Chicken
Heat oven to 400°F. Marinate chicken as above. Place chicken in roasting pan and roast until cooked through, about 45 minutes.

Chicken Korma with Broccoli and Toasted Almonds

This Indian dish, which would ordinarily take more than an hour to prepare, is made much easier with jarred sauce mix.

PREP TIME: 5 MINUTES • COOK TIME: 15 MINUTES • MAKES: 4 SERVINGS

3 tablespoons sliced almonds
1 tablespoon vegetable oil
1 ¼ pounds chicken tenders, cut crosswise
   ½ inch thick
1 jar (15 ounces) creamy coconut sauce
2 cups frozen broccoli cuts, thawed
Instant rice, prepared according to
   package directions

1. In a nonstick 12-inch skillet over medium heat, toast nuts until golden, shaking pan to keep them from burning, about 5 minutes. Transfer to a plate.

2. In the same pan over medium-high heat, heat oil. Add chicken and cook, stirring, 2 minutes. Add coconut sauce, broccoli, and ½ cup water, and bring to boiling. Reduce heat to medium and simmer until broccoli is tender, about 4 minutes.

3. Spoon rice onto a serving plate. Spoon chicken and sauce over and sprinkle almonds on top.

Chicken with Pears and Cream

This dish is a favorite for fall. I usually serve it with Baked Sweet Poatoes with Maple-Chipotle Butter (p. 154).

PREP TIME: 8 MINUTES • COOK TIME: 12 MINUTES • MAKES: 4 SERVINGS

4 large skinless boneless chicken breast halves (about 6 ounces each), trimmed of fat
Salt and freshly ground black pepper
2 tablespoons all-purpose flour
2 tablespoons extra-virgin olive oil
3 tablespoons leek soup mix
⅓ cup heavy cream
1 cup sliced canned pears in juice, drained

1. Season chicken with salt and pepper; sprinkle with flour.

2. In a large nonstick skillet over medium-high heat, heat oil. Add chicken and cook, turning once, until golden on both sides and just cooked through, 7 to 8 minutes. Transfer chicken to a plate and cover with foil to keep warm.

3. Add soup mix, cream, and 1 cup water to the pan and bring to boiling. Cook until the liquid is reduced by half, 3 to 4 minutes. Add pears and season with salt and pepper. Turn chicken in sauce to coat, then transfer to plates. Spoon sauce over chicken and serve immediately.

Chicken Legs and Peas in Pink Sauce

COOK TIME: 30 MINUTES • MAKES: 4 SERVINGS

1 tablespoon olive oil
8 chicken drumsticks
1 cup jarred tomato-basil pasta sauce
½ cup heavy cream
1 box (9 ounces) frozen baby peas

1. In a medium nonstick skillet over medium-high heat, heat oil. Add drumsticks and cook until browned, about 4 minutes. Transfer chicken to a plate; discard fat from pan. Add tomato sauce, cream, and ¼ cup water to pan. Return chicken to pan and bring to boiling. Reduce heat to medium, cover, and simmer, turning occasionally, until chicken is cooked through, about 25 minutes.

2. Meanwhile, cook peas in microwave according to package directions. Stir into finished sauce and serve immediately.

Oven-Fried Buffalo Wings

Liven up your next party with this dish. Frozen chicken wings make it really easy.

PREP TIME: 5 MINUTES • COOK TIME: 50 MINUTES • MAKES: 4 TO 8 SERVINGS

48 ice-glazed frozen chicken wing
    segments
¼ cup cayenne-pepper hot sauce
Bottled blue cheese dressing, for serving
2 packages (8 ounces each) carrot and
    celery sticks, for serving

1. Place racks in top and lower third of oven and heat oven to 450°F.

2. Line 2 baking sheets with foil and spray with vegetable oil cooking spray. Arrange 24 wing segments on each pan. Place pans in top and bottom of oven and roast 30 minutes. Switch pans and cook 20 minutes more, until skin is crisp.

3. Using tongs, transfer wings to a large bowl, drizzle with pepper sauce, and toss until wings are coated. Serve with blue cheese dressing and vegetables on the side.

Chicken and Carrots in Lemon-Thyme Gravy

Potatoes (baked in the microwave) are a perfect accompaniment to this satisfying main dish.

PREP TIME: 10 MINUTES • **COOK TIME: 15 MINUTES** • **MAKES: 4 SERVINGS**

1 tablespoon olive oil
4 boneless skinless chicken breast halves
  (about 6 ounces each), trimmed of fat
1 packet (1.2 ounces) roasted chicken
  gravy mix
¾ cup milk
¼ cup lemon juice (fresh or bottled)
½ teaspoon dried thyme
1 box (9 ounces) frozen baby carrots

1. In a 12-inch nonstick skillet over medium-high heat, heat oil. Add chicken and cook, turning once, until browned, about 4 minutes.

2. While chicken is cooking, in a medium bowl, whisk together gravy mix, milk, lemon juice, thyme, and 1 cup water. Transfer chicken to a plate, add sauce to pan and bring to a boil, whisking. Return chicken and any juices to pan, reduce heat to medium-low, and simmer, turning chicken occasionally, until chicken is cooked through, about 10 minutes.

3. Meanwhile, cook carrots in microwave according to package directions. Stir carrots into sauce, and serve with chicken.

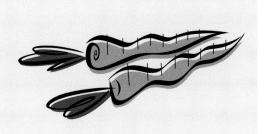

Lemony Turkey London Broil

Boneless turkey breasts are perfect for grilling for a crowd in a short amount of time. You can easily double the recipe to make 12 servings. Pick up prepared side dishes from your supermarket deli, throw together a green salad, and you're all set for dinner!

PREP TIME: 1¼ HOURS • COOK TIME: 45 MINUTES • MAKES: 6 SERVINGS

1 small onion, finely chopped
1 tablespoon jarred minced garlic
1 teaspoon salt-free lemon-pepper seasoning
½ cup olive oil
⅓ cup fresh lemon juice
½ teaspoon salt
1 boneless turkey breast half (about 2¼ pounds)

1. In a large nonreactive bowl, whisk together onion, garlic, lemon pepper, oil, lemon juice, and salt. Add turkey, turn to coat, cover and chill for 1 to 3 hours.

2. Heat gas grill at medium flame or arrange charcoal in a circular fashion for indirect heat. Remove turkey from marinade, place on grill, cover, and cook, turning once and rotating roast as necessary, until skin is golden and an instant thermometer inserted in center reaches 155°F, about 45 minutes.

3. Remove from heat and let stand 5 minutes. To serve, carve thinly against the grain.

Strip Steaks with Broccoli and Spicy Orange Sauce

This dish is inspired by Orange Beef, a traditional offering at many Chinese restaurants. Here the sauce is lighter, with a refreshing dash of orange and the addition of crisp-tender broccoli.

PREP TIME: 10 MINUTES • COOK TIME: 15 MINUTES • MAKES: 4 SERVINGS

4 trimmed boneless New York strip steaks
   (9 to 10 ounces each)
Salt and freshly ground black pepper
2 tablespoons all-purpose flour
2 tablespoons safflower oil
1 cup beef broth
½ teaspoon red pepper flakes
1 bag (1 pound) frozen cut broccoli,
   thawed
1 tablespoon orange marmalade
2 teaspoons Asian (dark) sesame oil

1. Season steaks with salt and pepper and sprinkle with flour.

2. In a large heavy skillet over medium-high heat, heat oil. Add steaks and cook, turning once, 6 minutes total for medium-rare. Transfer to a cutting board and cover loosely with foil to keep warm.

3. Add broth and pepper flakes to skillet and bring to boiling. Cook until liquid is reduced by half, about 4 minutes. Stir in marmalade and broccoli and cook until heated through, about 2 minutes. Remove from heat and stir in sesame oil.

4. Slice steaks into ⅓-inch-thick slices and spoon sauce on top.

Quick Sesame Beef and Broccoli

For an Asian-inspired change of pace, serve this stir-fry over buckwheat soba noodles instead of rice.

PREP TIME: 5 MINUTES • COOK TIME: 10 MINUTES • MAKES: 4 SERVINGS

1 tablespoon sesame seeds
2 tablespoons vegetable oil
1 New York strip steak or boneless shell steak (1 pound), sliced crosswise $\frac{1}{4}$ inch thick
1 pound fresh broccoli cuts, rinsed
$\frac{1}{3}$ cup stir-fry sauce
1 can (8 ounces) sliced water chestnuts, rinsed and drained

1. In a nonstick 12-inch skillet over medium-high heat, toast sesame seeds until golden, 1 to 2 minutes. Transfer to a plate.

2. Add oil to pan and increase heat to high. Add steak slices and cook, turning once or twice, until no longer red, 1 to 2 minutes. Transfer to a bowl.

3. Add broccoli, stir-fry sauce, and $\frac{1}{2}$ cup water to the skillet and cook, stirring occasionally, until broccoli is crisp-tender, about 4 minutes. Return meat to pan and add water chestnuts. Stir 1 minute to heat through. To serve, spoon mixture into a serving bowl and sprinkle with sesame seeds.

Beef-za

The best of both worlds—it's a pizza and a juicy hamburger in one. The cooking directions below are for meat that is fully cooked; for medium, don't cover the pan with a lid while cooking on top of stove. Serve with a green salad and toasted pita.

PREP TIME: 10 MINUTES • COOK TIME: 15 MINUTES • MAKES: 4 SERVINGS

1½ pounds lean ground beef
⅓ cup jarred tomato-basil pasta sauce
1 cup (4 ounces) shredded mozzarella cheese
Pinch dried oregano
¼ teaspoon red pepper flakes (optional)

1. Heat broiler. Pat meat into a 7-inch round, about ¾ inch thick.

2. Lightly oil a 9- to 10-inch ovenproof skillet (cast iron works great) and heat over medium heat until hot. Carefully add beef patty to pan, cover, and cook 8 minutes. Uncover, transfer pan to broiler, and cook 4 minutes longer.

3. Spread sauce evenly on top of patty, leaving a 1-inch border all around. Put cheese on top of sauce and sprinkle with oregano and pepper flakes. Broil until cheese is lightly browned and bubbly, 2 to 3 minutes. To serve, cut into wedges.

Oven-Roasted Filet Mignon

This aromatic-spiced whole filet is surpisingly simple and quick to prepare—perfect for an elegant dinner party. Serve with Gingered Potatoes (p. 140) and Roasted Broccoli with Garlic (p. 151) or Soy-Roasted Green Beans.

PREP TIME: 10 MINUTES • ROAST TIME: 20 MINUTES • MAKES: 10 TO 12 SERVINGS

1 jar (9 ounces) ginger and garlic
   marinade
1 tablespoon vegetable oil
1 whole trimmed filet of beef (about 18
   inches long, 4½ to 5 pounds)

1. Heat oven to 500°F or prepare grill. Grease a large roasting pan.

2. Combine marinade and oil. Place beef in pan and brush with marinade.

3. Roast filet in pan in oven or cook meat directly on medium-high grill for 10 minutes. Using tongs, turn meat over and cook until internal temperature reaches 130°F on an instant-read thermometer, about 10 minutes more.

4. Transfer to a cutting board with grooves and let stand 5 minutes before slicing. Serve either sliced on a large platter or in individual portions.

Sirloin Steak au Poivre

Serve this hearty dish, with lots of gravy, with Zippy Oven Fries (p. 157) or baked potatoes. Be careful when adding the brandy—it will flame up, so keep any towels (or body parts) away from the pan.

PREP TIME: 5 MINUTES • COOK TIME: 25 MINUTES • MAKES: 6 SERVINGS

1 boneless sirloin steak (about 2 inches thick, 2 ½ pounds)
Freshly ground black pepper
2 tablespoons extra-virgin olive oil
3 tablespoons green peppercorns in brine, drained
¼ cup brandy
1 packet (1 ounce) gravy mix
½ cup heavy cream

1. Pat steak dry and sprinkle generously with pepper.

2. In a large heavy skillet over medium-high heat, heat oil until hot but not smoking. Add steak and cook, turning once, 18 to 20 minutes total for medium-rare. Transfer to a cutting board and cover loosely with foil while you prepare sauce.

3. Reduce heat to medium. Add green peppercorns and brandy to skillet. Carefully shake pan until flame dies down. Add gravy mix, cream, and 1 ½ cups water. Whisk until boiling and cook until sauce has thickened, about 5 minutes.

4. Slice steak into ⅓-inch-thick slices and arrange on plates. Spoon sauce over steak and serve.

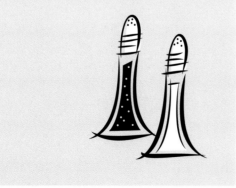

Grilled Steak with Cheddar Sauce

Side dishes of steamed broccoli and baked potatoes will benefit from this easy cheese sauce.

PREP TIME: 15 MINUTES • COOK TIME: 30 MINUTES • MAKES: 4 TO 6 SERVINGS

1 boneless sirloin or top or bottom round
   London broil (2 $\frac{1}{2}$ to 3 pounds)
Salt and freshly ground black pepper
2 tablespoons unsalted butter
$\frac{3}{4}$ cup frozen chopped onion
2 tablespoons all-purpose flour
1 $\frac{1}{2}$ cups milk
2 cups (8 ounces) shredded cheddar
   cheese

1. Prepare a grill or heat broiler. Season steak lightly with salt and pepper. Grill or broil steak uncovered, turning once, 16 to 18 minutes for medium-rare.

2. Meanwhile, in a medium saucepan over medium heat, melt the butter. Add onion and $\frac{1}{2}$ teaspoon each salt and pepper and cook, stirring often, until soft, about 7 minutes. Stir in the flour and cook 2 minutes longer. Gradually whisk in milk and cheese and cook, whisking, until sauce is thick, about 5 minutes.

3. Transfer meat to a grooved cutting board. Let stand 5 minutes. Slice sirloin into $\frac{1}{3}$-inch-thick slices diagonally against the grain. Transfer meat to a serving platter and serve immediately with the warm cheese sauce on the side.

VARIATION

Grilled Steak with Blue Cheese Sauce
Substitute an equal amount of crumbled Roquefort or Gorgonzola for the cheddar.

Beef and Mushroom Skillet Supper

Once you have the ingredients for this dish assembled, it takes about 10 minutes to cook. Serve over toast or with buttered noodles.

PREP TIME: 5 MINUTES • COOK TIME: 10 MINUTES • MAKES: 4 SERVINGS

1 tablespoon olive oil
1 ½ pounds ground sirloin
½ cup frozen chopped onion
1 box (15 ounces) frozen cream of
   mushroom soup, thawed
2 teaspoons Worcestershire sauce
1 teaspoon Dijon mustard
⅓ cup sour cream

1. In a 12-inch nonstick skillet over medium high heat, heat oil. Add beef and cook, using a wooden spoon to break up meat, until browned, about 5 minutes. Carefully discard excess fat.

2. Add onion to pan and cook over medium heat, stirring, until softened, about 4 minutes. Add soup, Worcestershire, and mustard and bring to boiling. Stir in sour cream and remove from heat. Serve immediately.

Easiest Beef and Vegetable Stew

This dish hits the spot when you're in the mood for stew but don't have the time. Serve with mashed potatoes or instant polenta.

PREP TIME: 5 MINUTES • COOK TIME: 20 MINUTES • MAKES: 4 SERVINGS

1¼ pounds lean ground beef
1 medium onion, finely chopped
1 packet (1 ounce) brown sauce mix
1 tablespoon tomato paste
1 box (9 ounces) frozen green beans
1 cup frozen crinkle-cut carrots

1. In a nonstick 12-inch skillet over medium-high heat, cook ground beef, using a wooden spoon to break up meat, until browned, about 5 minutes. Add onion and cook over medium heat until softened, about 4 minutes.

2. In a medium bowl, combine sauce mix, tomato paste, and 1½ cups water. Add mixture to skillet. Stir in green beans and carrots and bring to boiling. Reduce heat to medium and simmer, stirring occasionally, until soup is thick and vegetables are tender, about 5 minutes.

Pepper-Stuffed Flank Steak

Before company comes, sauté the vegetables and marinate and stuff and sear the steak. After your guests have arrived, just pop the meat in the oven and cook some rice—it's so easy!

PREP TIME: 20 MINUTES • COOK TIME: 45 MINUTES • MAKES: 6 SERVINGS

2 tablespoons vegetable oil
1 bag (1 pound) frozen bell pepper and
   onion stir-fry strips
1 jar (4.5 ounces) sliced mushrooms,
   drained
3 tablespoons stir-fry sauce
1 teaspoon dry ginger
1 large flank steak (2½ to 3 pounds)
1 cup roasted red pepper-tomato pasta
   sauce
Kitchen twine

1. In a large ovenproof skillet over medium heat, heat 1 tablespoon oil. Add bell pepper and onion, mushrooms, stir-fry sauce, and ginger; cook, stirring, 4 minutes. Transfer to a plate and let cool. Arrange half of cooked vegetables lengthwise down the center of the steak. Roll steak around filling and tie with kitchen twine.

2. Heat oven to 400°F. Add remaining tablespoon of oil to skillet, add steak, and cook, turning, over medium-high heat, until seared, about 7 minutes. Transfer pan to oven and roast 30 minutes, until internal temperature reaches 130°F on an instant-read thermometer. Transfer steak to a cutting board with grooves. Add remaining vegetables and tomato sauce to skillet. Cook over medium heat until vegetables are very tender, about 4 minutes.

3. To serve, slice steak into ½-inch-thick slices. Arrange on plates and spoon sauce and any juices that have collected on the cutting board over.

Grilled Mini Meatloaves

Ketchup is the key ingredient for these smoky individual loaves that are quickly and easily cooked on the grill. Serve with mashed potatoes and a green vegetable.

PREP TIME: 15 MINUTES • COOK TIME: 10 MINUTES • MAKES: 4 SERVINGS

2 strips cooked bacon
1½ pounds lean ground sirloin
¾ cup plain dry breadcrumbs
⅓ cup onion soup mix
1 large egg plus 1 yolk
3 tablespoons ketchup, plus
    more for serving

1. Place bacon on a paper towel-lined plate and crisp in microwave 30 seconds. Transfer to a board and chop.

2. In a large bowl use your hands to mix together meat, breadcrumbs, soup mix, egg and yolk, 3 tablespoons ketchup, ½ cup water, and reserved bacon until blended. Divide into 4 portions and form into ⅔-inch-thick oval patties.

3. Prepare grill or heat a grill pan over medium heat. Add patties, cover, and cook, turning once or twice, until nicely charred and firm to touch, 8 to 10 minutes. Serve hot or cold with ketchup.

Peachy Pork Chops

In summer, grill the chops outside and serve with grilled fresh peach (or nectarine, if you like) halves. Serve with your choice of rice and Soy-Roasted Green Beans (p. 140).

PREP TIME: 10 MINUTES • COOK TIME: 20 MINUTES • MAKES: 4 SERVINGS

½ cup peach jam
1½ tablespoons soy sauce
8 (½-inch-thick) loin pork chops (2¼ pounds total)
4 canned peach halves, drained
2 tablespoons chopped fresh cilantro, for garnish

1. In a microwave-proof bowl, combine jam and soy sauce . Cook on high power for 1 minute; whisk until smooth and let cool 2 minutes. Add pork chops, turn to coat, and let stand 5 minutes.

2. Heat a grill pan over medium heat until hot, about 2 minutes. Add half the chops and cook, turning once, until just cooked through, 6 to 7 minutes; transfer to plates and cover with foil to keep warm. Repeat with remaining chops.

3. Add peach halves to pan and grill until marked and heated through, 3 to 4 minutes.

4. To serve, arrange 2 chops and 1 peach half on each plate. Sprinkle with cilantro.

VARIATION

Blackberry Chicken Breasts
Substitute 8 skinless boneless chicken breast halves for the pork chops and seedless blackberry jam for the peach jam. Prepare as directed above, increasing cook time to 7 to 9 minutes.

Sautéed Pork Florentine

This bright, lemony pork goes well with almost any potato, noodle or rice dish, but I especially like it with Creamy Dreamy Mashed Potatoes (p. 155) or Nutty Herbed Rice Pilaf (p. 166).

PREP TIME: 5 MINUTES • COOK TIME: 15 MINUTES • MAKES: 4 SERVINGS

1 piece boneless pork loin, cut crosswise
　　into 8 medallions (1¼ pounds)
Salt and freshly ground black pepper
2 tablespoons all-purpose flour
1 tablespoon olive oil
3 tablespoons onion soup mix
1 tablespoon fresh lemon juice
3 tablespoons unsalted butter
2 boxes (10 ounces each) frozen leaf
　　spinach, thawed and squeezed dry

1. Season pork lightly with salt and pepper; sprinkle both sides with flour.

2. In a 12-inch skillet over medium-high heat, heat oil until hot but not smoking. Add pork and cook 3 minutes, turn, and cook until just cooked through, about 3 minutes longer. Transfer to a platter and cover loosely with foil to keep warm.

3. Add soup mix, lemon juice, and 1 cup water to pan; bring to a boil. Cook until liquid is reduced by half, about 5 minutes. Stir in butter and spinach; cook until heated through. Return pork slices and any juices that have collected to pan. Turn slices in sauce to coat. To serve, arrange 2 pork slices on each plate and spoon sauce over.

VARIATION

Sole Florentine
Substitute four 6-ounce sole fillets for the pork. Prepare as directed above.

Stir-Fried Pork with Eggplant and Zucchini

This Asian-inspired dish is quick to prepare and utilizes vegetables that grow in abundance in many home gardens. Serve with rice.

PREP TIME: 5 MINUTES • **COOK TIME: 15 MINUTES** • **MAKES: 4 SERVINGS**

1 tablespoon safflower oil

1½ tablespoons minced garlic

1 pound ground pork

½ cup low-sodium chicken broth

2 tablespoons stir-fry sauce

2 small eggplants (1 pound total), quartered lengthwise and sliced ¼-inch thick

1 cup sliced zucchini

1 can (8 ounces) straw mushrooms, drained

Instant rice, prepared according to package directions

1. In a 12-inch nonstick skillet over medium-high heat, heat oil. Add garlic and stir 1 minute. Add pork and cook 2 minutes, using a wooden spoon to break up meat. Add broth and stir-fry sauce and bring to boiling. Boil 3 minutes.

2. Add eggplant and cook, stirring, 3 minutes. Add zucchini and mushrooms and cook until eggplant is broken down and sauce is thickened, about 3 minutes longer. Divide rice among serving plates and spoon pork mixture over. Serve immediately.

15-Minute Stir-Fry

Serve this leftovers-inspired dish over rice or spaghetti.

PREP TIME: 5 MINUTES • COOK TIME: 10 MINUTES • MAKES: 4 SERVINGS

1 tablespoon vegetable oil
1 medium onion, sliced
1 celery rib, sliced
1 can (8 ounces) sliced mushrooms,
   drained
1 can (8 ounces) sliced water chestnuts,
   drained
1 can (8 ounces) flower-cut baby corn,
   drained
⅓ cup ginger-soy stir-fry sauce
2 cups sliced cooked chicken, pork,
   or steak
1 can (8 ounces) bean sprouts, drained

In a nonstick 12-inch skillet over medium high heat, heat oil. Add onion and celery and stir-fry 2 minutes. Add mushrooms, water chestnuts, corn, and stir-fry sauce. Cook, stirring, until heated through, about 5 minutes. Add meat and bean sprouts and cook until heated through, about 2 minutes.

Polynesian Pork Chops

Serve these sweet and succulent chops with Fruited Pilaf (p. 166).

PREP TIME: 5 MINUTES • **COOK TIME: 10 MINUTES** • **MAKES: 4 SERVINGS**

3 tablespoons soy sauce
3 tablespoons ketchup
3 tablespoons honey
1 teaspoon jarred minced garlic
8 thin-cut loin pork chops

1. Heat broiler. Line a baking sheet with foil and spray with vegetable oil cooking spray.

2. In a cup, stir together soy sauce, ketchup, honey, and garlic. Arrange chops on prepared pan and brush on half of sauce.

3. Broil until browned, about 5 minutes. Turn chops and brush with remaining sauce. Broil until browned and cooked through, about 5 minutes longer.

VARIATION

Polynesian Chicken Legs
Brush sauce on chicken legs and bake at 400°F until cooked through, about 30 minutes. For crispy skin, broil for 2 minutes.

Herbed Marinated Lamb Chops

You can marinate these simple, delicious chops for 30 minutes or up to 2 days.

PREP TIME: 35 MINUTES • COOK TIME: 15 MINUTES • MAKES: 4 SERVINGS

¼ cup extra-virgin olive oil
2 tablespoons red wine vinegar
1 tablespoon jarred minced garlic
½ tablespoon dried Italian mixed herbs
8 loin lamb chops (1½ inches thick, about
   2⅓ pounds total)
Salt and freshly ground black pepper

1. Combine oil, vinegar, garlic, dried herbs, and ½ teaspoon pepper in a large plastic bag. Add chops, squeeze out excess air, and seal bag completely. Turn bag to coat chops with marinade and then chill 30 minutes.

2. Heat a grill pan over medium heat until hot but not smoking. Remove chops from marinade and season with salt and pepper. Place chops in pan, cover loosely with foil, and cook 7 minutes. Turn and cook, covered, 5 minutes longer for medium-rare. Transfer chops to plates and let stand 5 minutes before serving.

VARIATIONS

Herb-Marinated Veal Chops
Use 4 veal chops (¾ inch thick, about 10 ounces each). Prepare as directed above.

Herb-Marinated Chicken Breasts
Use 4 boneless chicken breast halves (7 ounces each). Marinate as directed above. Cook 6 to 7 minutes, turning once.

Indian-Spiced Grilled Lamb

Have your butcher bone a whole leg of lamb for you, cut it into sections and butterfly it for even cooking. If you use a larger piece of lamb, you'll need more spice mix. Serve with rice and Cool Cucumbers in Yogurt (p. 161).

PREP TIME: 10 MINUTES • COOK TIME: 20 MINUTES • MAKES: 4 SERVINGS

1 tablespoon tandoori spice mix
1 piece boneless leg of lamb (about 1¾ pounds)
1½ cups grape tomatoes, halved
½ cup plain yogurt
1 tablespoon chopped fresh mint
Salt and freshly ground black pepper

1. Heat a grill pan over medium heat until hot. Sprinkle spice mixture on both sides of lamb and cook over medium heat, turning occasionally, about 20 minutes for medium-rare. Transfer to a cutting board, cover loosely with foil, and let stand 5 minutes.

2. In a small bowl, stir together tomatoes, yogurt, and mint. Season to taste with salt and pepper. To serve, slice meat against the grain on the diagonal into thin slices, arrange on plates, and spoon yogurt mixture over.

VARIATION

Indian-Spiced Flank Steak
Substitute a 1½- to 2-pound flank steak for the lamb. Prepare as directed above.

Veal Tikka Masala

This exotic Indian braise is simple and delicious. If you want it spicier, add a dash of cayenne. Serve with rice and Indian Sauteéd Greens (p. 143).

PREP TIME: 5 MINUTES • COOK TIME: 20 MINUTES • MAKES: 4 SERVINGS

¼ cup safflower oil
2 pounds thin veal scaloppine
1 medium onion, finely chopped
2 cups packaged sliced mushrooms
1 jar (15 ounces) tikka masala sauce

1. In a nonstick 12-inch skillet over medium-high heat, heat 2 tablespoons oil. Add 3 or 4 slices veal (whatever will fit without crowding the pan), cook 1 minute, turn and cook 1 minute longer. Transfer to a plate, arranging in a single layer, and repeat with remaining veal. (Do not stack veal, or it will steam and overcook.)

2. Add onion and mushrooms to pan and cook over medium heat, stirring, until tender, about 7 minutes. Add sauce and bring to simmering. Return veal and any juices that have collected to skillet and cook, turning, just until heated through, 1 to 2 minutes.

5-Ingredient Baked Stuffed Shrimp

This dish can be served as a first course for eight or as an entrée for four. You can assemble the shrimp up to 6 hours ahead; cover and refrigerate until ready to bake.

PREP TIME: 15 MINUTES • COOK TIME: 12 MINUTES • MAKES: 4 TO 8 SERVINGS

Butter or oil for greasing baking sheet
8 ounces back-fin or lump crabmeat, picked over
1 cup (4 ounces) finely shredded Swiss cheese
⅓ cup mayonnaise
2 tablespoons plain dried breadcrumbs
Freshly ground black pepper
24 peeled and deveined jumbo shrimp (about 2 pounds), butterflied (split nearly in half lengthwise)
Lemon wedges, for serving

1. Heat oven to 400°F. Lightly grease a baking sheet.

2. In a medium bowl, combine crabmeat, cheese, mayonnaise, and breadcrumbs. Season with pepper and stir with a fork until well blended.

3. Arrange shrimp cut-side down on prepared baking sheet with tails curved over the top. Stuff 1 generous tablespoon of crab mixture into the center of each shrimp curl. Bake until shrimp are pink and firm and stuffing is hot, 10 to 12 minutes. Serve with lemon wedges.

Smothered Tuna

Served with garlic-flavored instant polenta, this is an elegant dinner for four.

PREP TIME: 5 MINUTES • COOK TIME: 40 MINUTES • MAKES: 4 SERVINGS

2 tablespoons extra virgin olive oil
4 tuna fillets (about ¾ inch thick, 6
   ounces each)
2 cups frozen sliced onion and bell pepper
   strips
1 can (14 ounces) crushed tomatoes
1 tablespoon roasted garlic soup mix
⅛ to ¼ teaspoon red pepper flakes

1. In a 12-inch nonstick skillet over medium-high heat, heat oil. Add tuna, cook until seared, about 2 minutes, turn, and cook 2 minutes more. Transfer tuna to a plate.

2. Add onion and bell pepper to pan and cook, stirring, until softened, about 5 minutes. Add crushed tomatoes, soup mix, pepper flakes, and 1 cup water and bring to a boil; reduce heat, and simmer until vegetables are tender and sauce is thickened, 20 to 25 minutes. Return tuna to pan and cook, turning once, until heated through, about 3 minutes.

VARIATIONS

Smothered Sausages
Substitute 1½ pounds sweet Italian sausages for the tuna. Pierce sausages with a fork. In a dry skillet over medium heat, pan-fry the sausages, turning, until firm and browned. Remove sausages from pan. Return sausages to pan when you add tomatoes, and add salt to taste. Continue as directed above.

Smothered Pork Chops
Substitute four boneless pork chops (6 to 8 ounces each). In a 12-inch nonstick skillet over medium-high heat, heat oil. Add pork, cook until just cooked through, 6 to 7 minutes. Continue as directed above.

Asian Crab Cakes

Serve these exotic crab cakes with pickled ginger and a crisp cucumber salad. Assemble the crab cakes up to 5 hours ahead and refrigerate on the baking sheet until ready to bake. Panko (Japanese breadcrumbs) can be found in Asian supermarkets.

PREP TIME: 30 MINUTES • COOK TIME: 16 MINUTES • MAKES: 4 SERVINGS

1 pound back-fin crabmeat, picked
    through to remove any shell pieces and
    flaked with a fork
½ cup wasabi mayonnaise
2 tablespoons soy sauce
2 tablespoons plus ½ cup dried
    breadcrumbs, preferably panko
2 tablespoons unsalted butter
1 teaspoon minced garlic
Salt and freshly ground black pepper
Lemon wedges, for serving

1. Combine crab, mayonnaise, and soy sauce and mix well with a fork. Stir in 2 tablespoons breadcrumbs and refrigerate 10 minutes.

2. In a small skillet over medium heat, melt butter with garlic. Add remaining ½ cup breadcrumbs and ¼ teaspoon each of salt and pepper, and cook, stirring occasionally, until golden brown, about 6 minutes. Transfer crumbs to a plate.

3. Heat oven to 400°F. Line a baking sheet with foil and grease lightly. Divide crab mixture into fourths and use your hands to form each fourth into a patty. Turn patties in cooled crumbs, patting to coat. Arrange cakes on pan, sprinkling any remaining crumbs on top. Bake until heated through, 8 to 10 minutes. Serve immediately with lemon wedges.

Outrageous Oven Scampi

Serve the shrimp as a main dish for four or an appetizer for six.

PREP TIME: 5 MINUTES • **COOK TIME: 15 MINUTES** • **MAKES: 4 TO 6 SERVINGS**

3 tablespoons unsalted butter
1 tablespoon jarred minced garlic
3 tablespoons extra-virgin olive oil
1½ pounds peeled and deveined large
  shrimp (about 30)
½ cup seasoned Italian-style breadcrumbs
Lemon wedges, for serving

1. Place oven rack in upper third of oven and heat oven to 400°F.

2. Slowly melt butter with garlic in a small saucepan over low heat. Remove from heat; stir in oil. When cool to the touch, stir 2 tablespoons garlic mixture into shrimp, then transfer shrimp to a 9-inch-square glass baking dish.

3. In a bowl, stir remaining garlic mixture into breadcrumbs. Sprinkle crumbs evenly over shrimp, and bake until shrimp are firm and orange, about 10 minutes. Serve with lemon wedges.

VARIATION

Scallop and Shrimp Scampi
Substitute cleaned sea scallops for half of the shrimp and prepare as directed above.

Best Pan-Fried Crispy Sole

Serve this light dish with a side of steamed spinach. The lemon wedges will add flavor both to the fish and greens.

PREP TIME: 25 MINUTES • **COOK TIME: 10 MINUTES** • **MAKES: 4 SERVINGS**

4 lemon sole fillets (8 ounces each)
2 tablespoons lemon juice
Salt and freshly ground black pepper
1 large egg
⅔ cup seasoned breadcrumbs
2 tablespoons extra-virgin olive oil
2 tablespoons unsalted butter
1 lemon, cut into wedges, for serving

1. Arrange fish on a plate. In a small bowl, stir together lemon juice and 2 tablespoons water. Drizzle mixture over fish. Sprinkle with ¼ teaspoon each of salt and pepper and let stand 15 minutes.

2. In a shallow bowl, beat together egg and ¼ cup water. Place breadcrumbs in another shallow bowl. Working with one fillet at a time, turn each fillet in egg and then in crumbs, patting and then shaking off excess.

3. In a 12-inch nonstick skillet over medium-high heat, heat 1 tablespoon each oil and butter. When butter is melted, add 2 pieces of fish and cook, turning once, until golden, 4 to 5 minutes. Transfer to plates and repeat with remaining fish. Serve immediately, garnished with lemon wedges.

Vegetable Fried Rice

This is a great way to utilize leftover rice!

PREP TIME: 5 MINUTES • **COOK TIME: 12 MINUTES** • **MAKES: 4 SERVINGS**

1½ cups frozen chopped onion
1 teaspoon jarred minced garlic
2 tablespoons vegetable oil
1 bag (1 pound) frozen stir-fry vegetables, thawed and chopped
3 large eggs, beaten
4 cups cooked white or brown rice
3 tablespoons stir-fry sauce

1. Cook onion and garlic in oil in a nonstick 12-inch skillet over medium-high heat, stirring, until golden, about 3 minutes. Add vegetables and stir-fry until tender, about 3 minutes.

2. Add eggs and stir-fry until firm, 1 to 2 minutes. Add rice and stir-fry sauce and cook, stirring, until heated through, about 5 minutes.

VARIATION

Shrimp Fried Rice
Add 2 cups cooked shelled and deveined medium shrimp along with the rice.

Pots of Gold

HomemadeTakeout-Chicken Noodle Soup

This recipe makes extra, which you can keep in the refrigerator for up to 4 days or freeze for up to 3 months.

PREP TIME: 10 MINUTES • COOK TIME: 20 MINUTES • MAKES: 6 TO 8 SERVINGS

1 roasted chicken (3 to 4 pounds)
1 carrot, finely chopped
1 large celery rib, finely chopped
2½ quarts low-sodium chicken broth
1½ cups fine egg noodles
Salt and freshly ground black pepper

1. Cut enough meat from chicken into large bite-size pieces to measure 3 cups. In a large saucepot, combine chicken, carrot, celery, and broth over medium heat. Bring to simmering and cook until vegetables are tender, about 20 minutes.

2. Meanwhile, cook noodles according to package instructions. Drain and stir into soup. Season to taste with salt and pepper and serve.

VARIATION

Stracciatelle
Omit egg noodles and substitute 2 boxes (10 ounces each) frozen chopped spinach, thawed and squeezed to remove excess moisture. Prepare as directed above. Just before serving, drizzle 3 beaten eggs into soup, stirring constantly.

Lemony Chicken and Mushroom Stew

This delicious stew is super-easy, made with a supermarket rotisserie chicken. Serve over rice or, for an elegant presentation, in baked puff pastry shells.

PREP TIME: 5 MINUTES • COOK TIME: 10 MINUTES • MAKES 6 TO 8 SERVINGS

2 tablespoons butter
1 package (10 ounces) sliced fresh
    mushrooms
1 ½ tablespoons flour
½ cup frozen chopped onion
1 box (1.4 ounces) leek soup mix
1 ½ teaspoons finely grated lemon zest
2 cups half-and-half
6 cups shredded cooked chicken
Salt and freshly ground black pepper

1. In a large saucepan over medium heat, melt the butter. Add mushrooms and onion and cook, stirring, 5 minutes. Stir in flour and cook, stirring, 2 minutes.

2. Stir in soup mix and lemon zest; gradually whisk in 1 cup water, then add half-and-half, about ½ cup at a time, whisking and letting mixture thicken after each addition. Bring to boiling, then cook, whisking, 2 minutes.

3. Stir in chicken and cook until heated through. (Can be made ahead, covered and refrigerated up to 2 days. Reheat over medium heat, stirring, until heated through.) Season to taste with salt and pepper and serve immediately.

Chicken Stew with Olives

Blanching the olives removes their saltiness and lets their subtle flavor come through. Serve with crusty bread and 1-2-3 House Salad (p. 160).

PREP TIME: 15 MINUTES • COOK TIME: 1 HOUR • MAKES: 4 SERVINGS

⅓ pound pitted green olives, rinsed
4 chicken leg quarters, separated at the joint
Salt and freshly ground black pepper
¼ cup all-purpose flour
2 tablespoons extra-virgin olive oil
1 box (9 ounces) frozen pearl onions, thawed
½ cup dry vermouth or white wine
1½ cups low sodium chicken broth
2 tablespoons chopped fresh parsley, for garnish (optional)

1. Bring a small saucepan of water to boiling, add olives, and cook 2 minutes. Drain, rinse with cold water, and repeat. If olives are still salty, repeat once more, then set aside.

2. Sprinkle chicken with salt and pepper. In a large sealable bag, combine chicken and flour. Seal completely and shake to coat chicken.

3. In a large deep skillet over medium heat, heat oil. Add chicken and cook, turning once or twice, until golden, about 6 minutes. Transfer pieces to a plate.

4. Add onions to skillet and cook until golden, about 6 minutes. Add vermouth and stir until evaporated, 2 to 3 minutes. Add broth, 1 cup water, and reserved olives and bring to boiling. Return chicken and any juices that have collected to skillet. Cover and simmer until chicken is very tender, about 50 minutes. To serve, transfer chicken to a serving platter. Skim fat from surface of sauce, then spoon sauce over chicken. Sprinkle with parsley, if desired, and serve.

Nutty Chicken Casserole

Serve this dish with rice and a green salad.

PREP TIME: 15 MINUTES • BAKE TIME: 30 MINUTES • MAKES: 4 TO 6 SERVINGS

Butter for greasing dish
3 cups sliced cooked chicken
1 box (15 ounces) frozen cream of
　　mushroom soup, thawed
1 cup salted roasted cashews
½ cup low-sodium chicken broth
1 cup finely chopped celery
1 cup frozen chopped onion
2 cups wide chow mein noodles

1. Place rack in lower third of the oven and heat the oven to 350°F. Butter a 9-inch-square glass baking dish.

2. In a large bowl, combine chicken, soup, cashews, broth, celery, and onion and toss until mixed. Transfer to prepared dish. Sprinkle chow mein noodles on top and bake until heated through, about 30 minutes.

Quick Chicken 'n' Dumplings

This light and hearty stew was inspired by my friend Susan Jaslove, a long-time recipe developer who now teaches middle-school students cooking and nutrition.

PREP TIME: 5 MINUTES • COOK TIME: 50 MINUTES • MAKES: 4 SERVINGS

8 skinless chicken thighs (3½ pounds total)
2 cups low-sodium chicken broth
½ teaspoon dried thyme
1 box (9 ounces) frozen pearl onions
1 cup bagged baby carrots
2 celery ribs, thinly sliced
1 box (10 ounces) frozen leaf spinach, thawed
Salt and freshly ground black pepper
1 cup self-rising cake flour
½ cup yellow cornmeal
3 tablespoons cold unsalted butter, cut into bits
⅔ cup milk

1. In a large saucepot over medium-high heat, combine chicken, broth, 2 cups water, and thyme. Bring to boiling. Reduce heat to medium, cover, and simmer 15 minutes. Add onions, carrots, and celery and simmer, covered, until vegetables are tender and chicken is cooked through, about 15 minutes longer. Stir in spinach and season with salt and pepper. Remove from heat, cover, and keep warm.

2. In a medium bowl, whisk together flour and cornmeal. Add butter and rub mixture with fingertips until crumbly. Stir in milk. Drop heaping tablespoons of batter on top of chicken stew. Cover and cook over medium-low heat until dumplings are cooked through, 10 to 12 minutes. To serve, ladle into shallow soup bowls and serve immediately.

Chicken Cacciatore

Serve this traditional Italian dish with a side of your favorite pasta and a green salad.

PREP TIME: 10 MINUTES • COOK TIME: 30 MINUTES • MAKES 4 SERVINGS

1 tablespoon olive oil
4 large chicken breast halves (with bones)
2 medium onions, thinly sliced
2 cups frozen bell pepper strips
1 teaspoon dried rosemary
1¼ cups porcini and tomato pasta sauce
¾ cup low-sodium chicken broth
Grated Parmigiano Reggiano cheese, for
   serving

1. In a heavy 12-inch or 10-inch deep skillet over medium-high heat, heat oil. Add chicken skin-side down and cook until browned, about 3 minutes. Turn and cook 2 minutes longer.

2. Add remaining ingredients (except for the grated cheese) to skillet and turn chicken to coat. Bring to boiling. Reduce heat to medium, cover, and simmer, turning occasionally, until vegetables are tender and chicken is cooked through, about 20 minutes. To serve, place each chicken breast on a serving plate and spoon sauce over. Sprinkle each serving with cheese and serve with additional cheese on the side.

Turkey Shepherd's Pie

This is a quintessential one-pot meal.

PREP TIME: 10 MINUTES • COOK TIME: 50 MINUTES • MAKES 4 TO 6 SERVINGS

Butter for greasing dish
1 package (24 ounces) blanched diced
   potatoes
⅔ cup heavy cream
Salt and freshly ground black pepper
4 cups sliced and coarsely chopped
   cooked turkey
1 box (10 ounces) frozen French-cut
   green beans, thawed and chopped
1 cup frozen crinkle-cut carrots, thawed
   and chopped
1 cup jarred gravy

1. Heat oven to 400°F. Butter a 9-inch-square glass baking dish.

2. Place potatoes in a large saucepan with cold water to cover and bring to boiling over high heat. Reduce heat to medium and cook until tender, 8 to 10 minutes. Drain, return potatoes to saucepan, and mash. Beat in cream. Season with salt and pepper.

3. In a medium bowl, stir together turkey, beans, carrots, and gravy. Transfer to baking dish and spread into an even layer. Spoon potatoes over and use the back of the spoon to smooth the top. Bake until golden, 25 to 30 minutes.

Turkey Potpie

These pies have a sweet cornbread crust on top. Be sure to place hot ramekins on top of plates to serve. Serve with Collard Greens with Ham (p. 144).

PREP TIME: 15 MINUTES • BAKE TIME: 20 MINUTES • MAKES: 4 SERVINGS

Butter
3 cups finely chopped cooked turkey
1 box (10 ounces) frozen peas and
　　carrots, thawed
1 cup gravy
¼ teaspoon thyme
Salt and freshly ground black pepper
1 box (7.5 ounces) cornbread mix

1. Heat oven to 400°F. Butter 4 large (8- to 10-ounce) ramekins or custard cups and place on a baking sheet.

2. In a medium saucepan over medium heat, combine turkey, peas and carrots, gravy, and thyme. Bring to simmering. Season with salt and pepper and spoon into ramekins.

3. Prepare cornbread mix according to package directions, substituting melted butter for the oil. Spoon batter on top of turkey mixture in ramekins, spreading evenly. Bake until cornbread is cooked through, about 20 minutes.

Turkey and Broccoli Galettes

This recipe makes two open-faced tarts .You can assemble them on separate baking sheets and freeze one, wrapped in foil, to bake up to two weeks later. Thaw frozen tart in fridge overnight and then bake as directed.

PREP TIME: 20 MINUTES • BAKE TIME: 50 MINUTES • MAKES: 2 TARTS

1 box (15 ounces) refrigerated pie crusts
1/2 cup milk
4 ounces cream cheese
1 package (1 pound) frozen chopped
  broccoli
1 1/2 cups shredded cheddar cheese
1 1/2 cups shredded cooked turkey meat

1. Bring crusts to room temperature.

2. Meanwhile, combine milk and cream cheese in a nonstick medium skillet and cook over medium heat, stirring, until smooth. Add broccoli and stir until warm. Remove from heat, stir in cheddar cheese and turkey and season to taste. Let cool.

3. Heat oven to 400°F. Place crusts side by side on a large baking sheet. Spoon 2 cups cooled filling into center of each, spreading to 1 1/2 inches from edge. Fold edge of pastry over filling, overlapping dough in folds as necessary.

4. Bake in center of oven 45 to 50 minutes. Let cool 10 minutes, then cut into wedges.

Turkey-Vegetable Black Bean Chili

This chili is delicious with the traditional garnishes of sour cream and cheddar, but soft fresh goat cheese is a tangy alternative that I love.

PREP TIME: 5 MINUTES • COOK TIME: 50 MINUTES • MAKES: 4 TO 6 SERVINGS

2 tablespoons safflower oil

1 package (1⅓ pounds) ground (dark and white meat) turkey

2 cups frozen chopped onion and bell pepper

2 teaspoons jarred minced garlic

1½ teaspoons chili powder

1 zucchini, sliced lengthwise and finely diced

1 can (14.5 ounces) diced tomatoes in thick juice

1 cup low-sodium chicken broth

1 can (15.5 ounces) black beans, rinsed and drained

1 box (9 ounces) frozen chopped spinach, thawed

1. In a 4-quart saucepot over medium-high heat, heat oil. Add turkey and cook, using a wooden spoon to break up meat until crumbly, about 6 minutes. Using a slotted spoon, transfer turkey to a plate.

2. Add onion and bell pepper, garlic, and chili powder to saucepot and cook, stirring, until softened, about 6 minutes. Stir in zucchini, tomatoes and their liquid, broth, and 1 cup water. Bring to boiling. Add beans, reduce heat to medium, and simmer uncovered until thickened, 25 to 30 minutes.

3. Meanwhile, place spinach in a colander and press with your hands to remove as much liquid as possible. Just before serving, stir spinach into the chili.

Turkey Enchiladas Verdes

Recaito is a Mexican seasoning paste made from cilantro, green chiles, garlic, and onions. If you can't find jars of it on the shelf, look for plastic containers of it in the frozen foods section. This casserole freezes nicely—simply thaw in the fridge before baking. This is a perfect post-Thanksgiving dish for leftover turkey.

PREP TIME: 20 MINUTES • COOK TIME: 30 MINUTES • MAKES: 6 SERVINGS

Butter or oil for greasing baking dish
12 fresh (soft) corn tortillas
2 jars (12 ounces each) recaito
3 cups shredded cooked turkey meat
2 cups (8 ounces) Mexican blend shredded
   cheese
½ cup thinly sliced onion
Sour cream, for serving

1. Heat oven to 350°F. Grease a 13 x 9-inch baking dish. Make 2 stacks of 6 tortillas and wrap each stack in foil. Place both packages in oven. Bake until tortillas are soft, about 5 minutes.

2. Reserve 1 cup recaito. In a medium bowl, combine turkey and remaining recaito.

3. Remove one package of tortillas from oven. Spoon ¼ cup turkey mixture on a tortilla, roll up, and place in prepared dish. Repeat with remaining turkey and tortillas. Spread reserved recaito over enchiladas and sprinkle with cheese and onion.

4. Increase oven temperature to 400°F. Bake enchiladas until cheese is melted and filling is heated through, about 30 minutes. Serve with sour cream on the side.

Turkey-Mushroom Casserole

Spoon this casserole into baked puff pastry shells or serve over toast or buttered noodles

PREP TIME: 20 MINUTES • BAKE TIME: 20 MINUTES • MAKES: 4 SERVINGS

2 tablespoons butter
1 cup frozen chopped onion
1 package (10 ounces) sliced cremini
   mushrooms
1 cup heavy cream
2 cups shredded cooked turkey
2 cups frozen broccoli cuts, thawed
¼ cup grated Parmesan cheese
Salt and freshly ground black pepper

1. Heat oven to 400°F. In a 12-inch nonstick skillet over medium heat, melt butter. Add onion and mushrooms and cook, stirring, until softened, about 5 minutes. Add cream and simmer until liquid has turned light brown and is reduced by half, about 6 minutes.

2. Stir in turkey, broccoli, and 2 tablespoons Parmesan. Season with salt and pepper. Transfer to a 1½- to 2-quart shallow casserole. Sprinkle with remaining 2 tablespoons Parmesan. (Can be made ahead, covered, and refrigerated overnight.) Bake until browned and bubbling, about 20 minutes.

Turkey-Mushroom Barley Soup

Be sure to allow time to either soak the barley overnight or use the quick-soak method indicated on the bag.

PREP TIME: 10 MINUTES • COOK TIME: 45 MINUTES • MAKES: 3 QUARTS (6 TO 8 SERVINGS)

1 cup pearl barley, rinsed and soaked
¼ ounce dried porcini mushrooms, rinsed
2 tablespoons safflower oil
1 large onion, finely chopped
1 large celery rib, finely chopped
1 package (8 ounces) sliced cremini
   mushrooms
1 quart low-sodium chicken broth
2 cups chopped cooked turkey
Sour cream and chopped fresh dill, for
   serving (optional)

1. Drain the barley. In a glass measuring cup, combine the porcini and 1 cup water. Microwave on high power 1 minute.

2. In a 4- to 6-quart saucepot over medium heat, heat oil. Add onion and celery and cook, stirring, 5 minutes. Add cremini mushrooms and cook until golden, about 4 minutes. Add broth, barley, and 4 cups water. Bring to boiling.

3. Meanwhile, remove soaked porcini from their liquid. Finely chop and add to saucepot, along with mushroom soaking liquid, pouring carefully to leave behind the grit in the bottom of the cup. Add turkey and simmer over medium-low heat until barley is tender, about 30 minutes. Serve with sour cream and a sprinkling of chopped fresh dill, if desired.

Roast Beef Hash

Leftover Top Round of Beef Roasted Over Vegetables (p. 91) is perfect to use in this hash. Top with poached or fried eggs for a hearty breakfast.

PREP TIME: 5 MINUTES • COOK TIME: 15 MINUTES • MAKES: 4 TO 6 SERVINGS

2 tablespoons olive oil
1½ cups frozen chopped onion
2 cups diced roast beef
2 tablespoons butter
4 leftover baked potatoes, peeled and
   diced (4 cups)
Salt and freshly ground black pepper

1. In a nonstick or cast-iron skillet over medium heat, heat the oil. Add onion and cook, stirring often, until golden, about 4 minutes. Add beef and cook until no longer pink. Transfer to a plate.

2. Add butter to the skillet. Add potatoes and cook over medium-high heat, turning infrequently, until browned and crusty, about 6 minutes. Return beef mixture to pan and cook until heated through, about 2 minutes. Season with salt and pepper.

VARIATION

Turkey Hash
Substitute 2 cups diced cooked turkey for the beef.

Quick and Hearty Beef Minestrone

This soup is perfect for lunch or dinner, especially on a chilly weekend. Add a sprinkling of Parmigiano Reggiano and serve garlic bread alongside.

PREP TIME: 10 MINUTES • COOK TIME: 50 MINUTES • MAKES: 2½ QUARTS (5 TO 6 SERVINGS)

1 tablespoon extra-virgin olive oil
1½ pounds boneless beef chuck or round,
    cut into ½-inch dice
1 bunch scallions, trimmed and thinly
    sliced
1 carrot, finely chopped
1 can (14.5 ounces) diced tomatoes with
    roasted garlic
2 cups beef broth
¾ cup ditalini (or other small tube pasta)
1 package (10 ounces) frozen cut green
    beans, thawed
1 can (15.5 ounces) small red beans,
    rinsed and drained
Salt and freshly ground black pepper

1. In a 4-quart saucepot over medium heat, heat oil. Add half the beef and cook, stirring occasionally, until browned, about 5 minutes. Transfer meat to a plate. Repeat with remaining meat, then return first batch of meat to saucepot. Add scallions, carrot, tomatoes, broth, and 2 cups water. Bring to a boil, reduce heat to medium-low, and simmer gently until meat is tender, about 30 minutes.

2. Meanwhile, cook ditalini according to package directions. Once meat is tender, add green beans, red beans, pasta, and 2 cups of the cooking water to saucepot. Cook until heated through, about 5 minutes. Season to taste with salt and pepper and serve.

Quick 'n' Spicy Beefy Chili

To make this chili spicier, I like to stir in one minced fresh jalapeño just before serving. Be sure taste the jalapeño before adding because they range from mild to fiery.

PREP TIME: 5 MINUTES • COOK TIME: 50 MINUTES • MAKES: 2½ QUARTS (6 TO 8 SERVINGS)

1 tablespoon safflower oil
2½ pounds ground sirloin or ground chuck
2 cups frozen chopped onions
1 tablespoon jarred minced garlic
2 tablespoons taco seasoning
1 can (28 ounces) crushed tomatoes
1 cup beef broth
1 can (4.5 ounces) chopped green chiles
1 can (15.5 ounces) small red beans,
   rinsed and drained
1 jalapeño pepper, minced (plus more, if
   desired)
Salt and freshly ground black pepper
2 packages Mexican-blend shredded
   cheese, for serving
Thinly sliced scallions, for serving
Prepared guacamole, for serving
Sour cream, for serving

1. In a 4- to 6-quart saucepot over medium-high heat, heat oil. Cook half of beef, using a wooden spoon to break up meat, until browned, about 5 minutes. Transfer beef to a plate using a slotted spoon. Repeat with remaining beef.

2. Reduce heat to medium. Add onions, garlic, and taco seasoning to saucepot and cook, stirring, until onion is soft, about 5 minutes. Return beef to pan. Stir in tomatoes, broth, and ½ cup water and bring to boiling. Reduce heat to medium-low and simmer, stirring occasionally, until thickened, about 20 minutes. Stir in chilies and beans. Simmer 10 minutes more. Stir in minced jalapeño and season to taste with salt and pepper. Serve hot with shredded cheese, scallions, guacamole, and sour cream on the side.

Basic Beef Stew

Make a double batch of this stew and freeze some for future (even easier) dinners.

PREP TIME: 5 MINUTES • COOK TIME: 2 HOURS • MAKES: 2½ QUARTS (6 TO 8 SERVINGS)

2¼ pounds boneless beef stew meat
Salt and freshly ground black pepper
2 tablespoons all-purpose flour
2 tablespoons olive oil
2½ cups beef broth
1 tablespoon butter
1 box (10 ounces) frozen pearl onions,
   thawed
2 cups fresh baby carrots
2 medium parsnips, sliced ¼ inch thick

1. Sprinkle beef with salt and pepper, then dust with flour. In a 4-quart saucepot over medium heat, heat oil. Add half of beef and cook until browned all over, 6 to 8 minutes. Transfer beef to a plate. Repeat with remaining beef, then return first batch of beef to saucepot. Pour in broth and 1 cup water and bring to a boil, stirring often. Reduce heat to medium-low, cover, and simmer for 1 hour.

2. In a medium skillet over medium heat, melt butter. Add onions and cook, shaking pan occasionally, until golden, 4 to 5 minutes.

3. Add onions, carrots, and parsnips to saucepot and simmer until vegetables are tender, about 30 minutes. Season to taste.

West Indian-Style Roast Beef Skillet Supper

Roast beef or steak works well in this dish. Serve with rice.

PREP TIME: 5 MINUTES • COOK TIME: 20 MINUTES • MAKES: 4 SERVINGS

3 tablespoons safflower oil

1 package (24 ounces) blanched diced potatoes

1 jar (14.5 ounces) sweet peppers and coconut sauce

1 box (10 ounces) frozen baby peas, thawed

2½ cups thinly sliced cooked steak or roast beef

1. In a large nonstick skillet over medium heat, heat the oil. Add potatoes and cook, turning occasionally, until tender inside and crisp outside, about 10 minutes.

2. Add sauce, peas, and ⅔ cup water. Cook, stirring, over medium-high heat until mixture simmers, about 3 minutes. Add beef and stir until heated through, about 5 minutes.

Pulled Pork

Serve these saucy pork sandwiches with Chili Corn (p. 148) or Seedy Slaw (p. 162).

PREP TIME: 15 MINUTES • COOK TIME: 1½ HOURS • MAKES: 6 SERVINGS

8 to 10 cups coarsely diced roasted ham
   (about 3 pounds)
3 peeled garlic cloves
⅓ cup cider vinegar
⅔ cup ketchup
2 tablespoons brown sugar
1½ tablespoons Worcestershire sauce
1 tablespoon yellow mustard
6 hamburger buns, for serving

1. In a large saucepan over medium-high heat, combine ham, garlic, vinegar, and 3½ cups water. Bring to boiling, reduce heat to medium-low, and simmer, partially covered, until meat is falling apart, about 1½ hours. Drain, reserving cooking liquid.

2. Return meat to saucepan. Stir in ketchup, brown sugar, Worcestershire, and mustard. Cook, stirring, over medium heat, until sauce is blended and sugar is melted. Add more cooking liquid as desired for more sauce. To serve, split hamburger buns and divide among plates. Spoon pork mixture over bottom buns and cover with top buns.

Tostadas de Puerco

You can use boneless pork loin or pork tenderloin for these fun, crispy "sandwiches." Choose whichever brand and heat level of salsa you prefer.

PREP TIME: 20 MINUTES • COOK TIME: 5 MINUTES • MAKES 4 SERVINGS

4½ cups diced cooked pork
8 (6-inch) corn tostadas
½ cup sour cream
4 cups chopped romaine lettuce (about 6 ounces)
1½ cups Mexican-blend shredded cheese
Salsa, for serving

1. Cook pork in a heavy medium skillet over medium heat, stirring occasionally, until crusty, about 4 minutes. Remove from heat.

2. Spread each tostada with 1 tablespoon sour cream and top with ⅓ cup pork, ½ cup lettuce, and 3 tablespoons cheese. Serve with salsa on the side.

Pork Tenderloin Thai Curry

Curries from Thailand satisfy all the taste buds. Serve this dish with white or brown rice.

PREP TIME: 10 MINUTES • COOK TIME: 15 MINUTES • MAKES: 6 SERVINGS

1½ tablespoons safflower oil
2 medium onions, halved and sliced
1 large red bell pepper, cut into ¾-inch
   dice
1 packet (1.75 ounces) red curry base
2½ tablespoons light brown sugar
1½ tablespoons fish sauce
1 can (13.5 ounces) Thai coconut milk (do
   not shake)
2 pork tenderloins (1½ to 1¾ pounds
   total), sliced crosswise ⅓ inch thick
1 package (1 pound) frozen broccoli cuts,
   thawed

1. In a 4-quart saucepan over medium-high heat, heat oil. Add onions, pepper, and red curry base and cook, stirring, 3 minutes. Stir in brown sugar and fish sauce. Scoop the creamy top off the coconut milk and combine with ½ cup water in a small bowl. Add mixture to saucepan. (Discard clear liquid in bottom of can.) Bring to boiling.

2. Add sliced pork and cook, stirring, 4 minutes. Add thawed broccoli and cook, stirring, until broccoli is hot and pork is just cooked through, 1 to 2 minutes more.

Scotch Broth

Scotch broth was traditionally made with mutton, and while shoulder is a tastier cut for stewing, leg of lamb is easier to find and much leaner.

PREP TIME: 5 MINUTES PLUS SOAKING • COOK TIME: 2 HOURS • MAKES: 2 QUARTS

1 1/2 pounds boneless lamb stew meat, cut into 1-inch pieces
1 1/2 cups beef broth
1/2 cup pearl barley, rinsed and soaked according to package directions
1 1/2 cups frozen chopped onion
2 large celery ribs, thinly sliced
1 parsnip, thinly sliced
Salt and freshly ground black pepper
1 box (9 ounces) frozen peas and carrots, thawed

1. Place lamb in a 4-quart saucepot and add cold water to cover. Over medium-high heat, bring to boiling. Drain in a colander and rinse with cold water. Rinse out saucepot and return meat to it. Add broth and 2 quarts water and bring to boiling. Reduce heat and simmer 45 minutes.

2. Drain and rinse barley. Add onion, celery, and parsnip to pot with drained barley and 1/2 teaspoon salt and bring to simmering. Cover and simmer over medium-low heat until meat and barley are tender, about 45 minutes. Stir in peas and carrots, cook 2 minutes, and season to taste with salt and pepper.

Moroccan Lamb Stew with Butternut Squash

This fragrant stew is similar to a tagine, a Moroccan dish that is prepared in a special clay casserole. Serve this sweetly spiced stew over fluffy couscous.

PREP TIME: 10 MINUTES • COOK TIME: 30 MINUTES • MAKES: 4 TO 6 SERVINGS

1 tablespoon safflower oil
2 pounds lean ground lamb
1½ cups frozen chopped onion
1 teaspoon salt-free seasoning blend
Pinch each ground cloves, ground allspice, and cinnamon
1 packet (1 ounce) brown sauce mix
1 butternut squash (about 1½ pounds), peeled, seeded and cut into ¾-inch chunks
½ cup dark raisins or dried currants
1 can (15.5 ounces) chickpeas, rinsed and drained
Salt and freshly ground black pepper
Couscous, cooked according to package directions, for serving

1. In a 4-quart saucepot over medium-high heat, heat oil. Add half of lamb to saucepot and cook, using a wooden spoon to break up meat, until browned, about 5 minutes. Using a slotted spoon, transfer lamb to a plate and repeat with remaining lamb. Add onion to pan juices and cook 2 minutes. Add seasoning blend and spices and stir 1 minute.

2. In a small bowl, stir together sauce mix and 2 cups water. Add to saucepot and whisk until boiling. Return lamb to pot, add squash and raisins, and simmer, stirring often, until squash is tender, about 10 minutes. Stir in chickpeas and cook over medium heat until heated through. Season to taste with salt and pepper. Spoon over couscous and serve.

Sausage, Potato, and Egg Casserole

Mix this casserole ahead, cover, and refrigerate for up to 12 hours, then just pop it in the oven when you're ready. This a perfect dish to serve when your house is full of holiday guests.

PREP TIME: 20 MINUTES • BAKE TIME: 40 MINUTES • MAKES: 6 SERVINGS

Butter for greasing dish
1 package (24 ounces) blanched diced
    potatoes
8 fully cooked breakfast sausages, sliced
    crosswise ¼ inch thick
1 cup grated Swiss cheese
9 eggs
2 scallions, finely chopped (optional)
¾ teaspoon salt
¼ teaspoon freshly ground black pepper

1. Heat oven to 350°F. Butter a 9-inch-square glass baking dish.

2. Place potatoes in a large saucepan with cold water to cover. Bring to boiling over high heat. Reduce heat and simmer until tender, about 10 minutes. Drain and transfer potatoes to prepared pan. Sprinkle sausage and cheese over potatoes.

3. In a medium bowl, whisk together eggs, scallions, salt, and pepper and pour into pan.

4. Bake until golden and just set in center, 35 to 40 minutes. Let stand 5 minutes before serving.

Almost-Instant White Bean and Sausage Soup

You can make this soup several days ahead, and it freezes well too. If the soup becomes too thick, simply thin it with a little water. A side of steamed or sautéed greens marries well with this soup.

PREP TIME: 10 MINUTES • COOK TIME: 20 MINUTES • MAKES: 2 QUARTS (4 TO 8 SERVINGS)

½ pound kielbasa, quartered lengthwise
    and thinly sliced
2 tablespoons olive oil
1 large onion, finely chopped
1½ tablespoons jarred chopped garlic
2 cans (1 pound 13 ounces each) white
    beans, rinsed and drained
2 cups low-sodium chicken broth
¼ cup chopped parsley
Salt and freshly ground black pepper
Sour cream, for serving

1. In a 4-quart saucepot over medium heat, cook sausage until browned. Transfer to a bowl. Add oil, onion, and garlic to saucepot and cook, stirring, over medium-low heat until softened, about 5 minutes. Add beans and, using a potato masher, mash until about half of beans are mashed.

2. Stir in broth and bring to a simmer. Cook, stirring occasionally, to blend flavors, 15 minutes. Stir in parsley. Season to taste with salt and pepper. To serve, ladle into soup bowls and serve with sour cream on the side.

VARIATION

Black Bean Soup
Omit the white beans and the kielbasa. Substitute the same amounts of black beans and diced smoked ham. Prepare and serve as directed above.

Spaghetti-Pepperoni Pie

You can substitute any kind of leftover pasta for the spaghetti in this dish.

PREP TIME: 10 MINUTES • BAKE TIME: 30 MINUTES • MAKES: 4 SERVINGS

Butter for greasing dish
8 eggs
⅓ cup grated Parmesan cheese
¼ teaspoon salt
¼ teaspoon black pepper
4 cups cooked spaghetti (about half of a
   1-pound box)
1 jar (4.5 ounces) sliced mushrooms,
   drained
1 cup packaged sliced pepperoni
2 tablespoons butter, melted

1. Heat oven to 400°F. Butter a 9-inch-square glass baking dish.

2. In a large bowl, beat together eggs, cheese, salt, and pepper. Add spaghetti, mushrooms, and pepperoni. Mix until combined and transfer to prepared dish.

3. Drizzle butter over mixture and bake until golden and eggs are set, about 30 minutes.

Franks 'n' Baked Beans

You can serve these beans as a side dish with barbecued meats—simply omit the hot dogs and take the beans out of the oven after 45 minutes. Add hot sauce if you like your beans spicy.

PREP TIME: 5 MINUTES • COOK TIME: 1 HOUR • MAKES: 10 SERVINGS

5 slices cooked bacon, cut into 1-inch
   pieces
2 cups frozen chopped onion
5 cans (15.5 ounces each) pinto beans,
   rinsed and drained
½ cup molasses
½ cup light brown sugar
2 tablespoons yellow mustard
2 tablespoons Worcestershire sauce
10 hot dogs, whole or cut up

1. Heat the oven to 350°F. In a 4-quart ovenproof pot over medium heat, combine bacon and onion, stirring occasionally, until onion is golden, about 6 minutes. Stir in beans, molasses, brown sugar, mustard, and Worcestershire sauce. Bring to boiling, cover, and transfer to oven.

2. Bake, stirring once or twice, 45 minutes. Add hot dogs to beans, cover and bake 5 minutes more. Serve immediately.

Red Pepper Gazpacho with Mexican Shrimp Cocktail

This chilled soup makes use of jarred peppers, so you can enjoy it year round. Look for roasted peppers in olive oil with garlic for the best flavor and use the oil from the peppers to add more flavor to a vinaigrette (like 1-2-3 House Salad, p. 160).

PREP TIME: 25 MINUTES • MAKES 1 QUART (4 SERVINGS)

1 jar (12 ounces) roasted red peppers packed in olive oil, drained (reserve oil and store in the refrigerator for another use)

1 cucumber (8 ounces), peeled and seeded

2 cups vegetable juice cocktail

¾ pound cooked, shelled and deveined medium shrimp, tails removed, cut into ½-inch dice

1 jar (4 ounces) chopped green chiles

¼ cup minced red onion

2 tablespoons fresh lime juice

½ teaspoon salt

1 ripe Hass avocado

Goat cheese or sour cream, for garnish

1. In a blender container, combine red peppers, cucumber, and juice and purée until smooth. Strain purée through a fine mesh sieve into a large bowl and refrigerate. (Can be made ahead, covered, and refrigerated up to 2 days.)

2. Just before serving, in a medium bowl, toss together shrimp, chilies, onion, lime juice, and ½ teaspoon salt. Finely dice avocado and add to shrimp mixture, tossing gently.

3. To serve, mound shrimp mixture into 4 shallow soup bowls, then ladle soup around. Top with goat cheese or sour cream and serve immediately.

Shellfish-Potato Bisque

This heavenly soup gets its creamy thickness from puréed corn and potato. Serve with garlic bread for sopping up the creamy broth.

PREP TIME: 20 MINUTES • COOK TIME: 15 MINUTES • MAKES: 1½ QUARTS (4 TO 6 SERVINGS)

2 cups half-and-half

3 cups mashed potato flakes

1 teaspoon tomato paste

2 boxes (10 ounces each) frozen white corn, thawed

½ pound peeled and cleaned raw shrimp, cut into ½-inch dice

6 ounces back-fin or lump crabmeat, picked over

1 tablespoon dry sherry (optional)

¼ cup minced fresh chives

Salt and freshly ground black pepper

1. In a large saucepan over medium heat, whisk together half-and-half, potato flakes, tomato paste, and 1½ cups water. Cook, whisking, just until mixture boils. Reduce heat to medium-low and simmer, whisking, 5 minutes.

2. In the bowl of a food processor with the steel blade attached, purée thawed corn. Set a fine mesh sieve over saucepan. Carefully transfer corn purée from processor to sieve and strain, pressing on solids, into potato mixture. Discard solids. Bring to a simmer over medium heat. Stir in shrimp, crab, sherry, and chives. Cook, stirring, until shrimp is firm. Season to taste with salt and pepper.

Stewed Clams with Bacon, Tomato, and Zucchini

You can serve this dish—a cross between a soup and a stew—over linguini or with crusty bread for dunking in the succulent sauce.

PREP TIME: 10 MINUTES • COOK TIME: 25 MINUTES • MAKES: 4 SERVINGS

6 strips bacon, thinly sliced crosswise
2 tablespoons extra-virgin olive oil
½ cup frozen chopped onion
2 teaspoons jarred minced garlic
1 medium zucchini, thinly sliced
1 cup dry white wine
1 cup jarred arrabbiata sauce
1 cup bottled clam juice
3 dozen littleneck clams, scrubbed
2 tablespoons finely chopped fresh
   parsley, for garnish

1. In a 6-quart saucepot over medium heat, cook bacon, stirring, until crisp, about 5 minutes. Add olive oil, onion, and garlic, and cook, stirring, 5 minutes.

2. Add zucchini, white wine, arrabbiata sauce, clam juice, and clams. Cover and bring to boiling. Reduce heat and simmer, stirring occasionally, until clams open, about 10 minutes. To serve, divide clams among 4 shallow soup plates, spoon sauce over, and sprinkle with parsley. Serve immediately.

Tuna-Melt Casserole

For the full effect, top each serving with a mound of shredded romaine or baby greens.

PREP TIME: 15 MINUTES • COOK TIME: 30 MINUTES • MAKES: 4 TO 6 SERVINGS

Salt
2 cups medium shells
6 ounces cream cheese, softened
1 can (6 ounces) solid white tuna in water,
    drained and flaked
2 scallions, thinly sliced
½ teaspoon freshly ground black pepper
1 cup grape tomatoes, cut in half
½ sleeve saltines, crushed
1 cup shredded cheddar cheese

1. Heat oven to 375ºF. Butter a 2-quart shallow baking dish.

2. In a large saucepot over high heat, bring 2 quarts of water to boiling. Add salt and the shells. Cook, stirring often, 5 minutes. Transfer 1 cup cooking water to a medium bowl, add cream cheese, and whisk until smooth. Continue cooking shells until al dente, 2 to 3 minutes more. Drain and return to saucepot.

3. Add the cream cheese mixture, tuna, scallions, and pepper. Toss until mixed and transfer to prepared dish. Sprinkle tomato halves on top. Bake until heated through, about 10 minutes. In a medium bowl, mix crushed saltines and cheese. Sprinkle on top of casserole and bake until cheese is melted, 10 minutes longer.

3-Ingredient Macaroni and Cheese

You can assemble this casserole a day ahead. Cover and refrigerate overnight, then bake as directed below. Serve with Sauteéd Peas with Lemon (p. 150).

PREP TIME: 20 MINUTES • COOK TIME: 30 MINUTES • MAKES: 4 SERVINGS

2 cups gemelli, fusilli, or other corkscrew
  pasta
6 ounces cream cheese, softened
1¾ cups shredded cheddar or cheddar-
  Jack cheese
Salt and freshly ground black pepper

1. Heat oven to 400°F. In a large saucepot over high heat, bring 2 quarts water to boiling. Add salt to taste and the pasta. Cook, stirring often, 6 minutes. Transfer 1 cup of cooking water to a medium bowl, add softened cream cheese, and whisk until smooth. Continue cooking pasta until al dente, 4 to 5 minutes longer.

2. Drain pasta and return it to the saucepot. Add the cream cheese mixture and 1¼ cups cheese and stir until smooth. Season with salt and pepper and transfer to a 9-inch-square glass baking dish. Sprinkle remaining ½ cup cheese on top.

3. Bake casserole until macaroni is heated through and cheese is golden, about 20 minutes.

VARIATION

Mexican Macaroni and Cheese
Stir 1 can (3.4 ounces) chopped green chilies and 1 large ripe tomato, diced, into the pasta after adding the cheese.

Love-It Lasagna

Just add garlic bread and a Caesar salad and you're set.

PREP TIME: 10 MINUTES • BAKE TIME: 25 MINUTES • MAKES: 4 SERVINGS

Butter for greasing dish
1 jar (26 ounces) tomato-basil pasta sauce
1 container (15 ounces) ricotta cheese
1 cup shredded mozzarella cheeese
¼ cup finely grated Parmesan cheese
2 large eggs
Freshly ground black pepper
12 (6-inch) egg roll wrappers

1. Heat oven to 400°F. Butter the bottom and sides of a 13 by 9-inch baking dish. Add 1 cup pasta sauce, tilting pan to coat bottom.

2. In a large saucepot over high heat bring 2 quarts of water to boiling. Fill a large bowl with cold water.

3. In a medium bowl, stir together ricotta, mozzarella, Parmesan, eggs, and ¼ teaspoon pepper.

4. Add 1 egg roll wrapper to boiling water and, using a slotted spoon, quickly transfer to cold water. Repeat with a second wrapper. Place wrappers flat, side by side, in bottom of baking dish. Top each with ½ cup cheese mixture. Cook 2 more wrappers and lay on top of cheese. Top each with ¼ cup pasta sauce.

5. Repeat layering twice: 2 wrappers, ½ cup cheese on each, 2 wrappers, ¼ cup sauce on each. Spoon any remaining tomato sauce on top and cover pan tightly with foil. Bake 25 minutes, remove from the oven and let stand uncovered 5 minutes before serving.

VARIATION

Love-It Vegetable Lasagna
Omit tomato-basil sauce and substitute mushroom-tomato or garden vegetable pasta sauce. Thaw and squeeze moisture out of a box (9 ounces) of chopped frozen spinach and add to the ricotta mixture. Prepare as directed above.

Eggplant Rollatine

Salting and draining the eggplant removes any bitterness, leaving behind only sweet and smoky eggplant flavor.

PREP TIME: 25 MINUTES • COOK TIME: 55 MINUTES • MAKES: 6 TO 8 SERVINGS

2 eggplants (8 ounces each), trimmed and thinly sliced lengthwise

Salt

1/3 cup olive oil, plus more for greasing foil

1 jar (26 ounces) marinara sauce

2 containers (15 ounces each) ricotta cheese

4 large eggs

1/2 cup grated Parmesan cheese

1/3 cup chopped fresh parsley (optional)

1/2 teaspoon freshly ground black pepper

1. Layer eggplant slices in a colander, sprinkling each layer lightly with salt; let stand in sink 15 minutes, then rinse eggplant and pat dry.

2. Heat broiler. Line a baking sheet with foil and lightly grease foil. Arrange 1/3 of eggplant on sheet in a single layer and brush with oil. Broil 3 minutes, turn and cook 3 minutes more, until tender. Transfer to a plate and repeat with remaining eggplant.

3. Butter a 15 x 10-inch baking dish and pour in marinara sauce. In a medium bowl, stir together ricotta, eggs, Parmesan, parsley, and pepper until well blended.

4. Lay several slices of eggplant on a work surface. Spoon a rounded tablespoon of cheese mixture on one end of each slice, roll up, and place side by side in prepared dish. Repeat with remaining eggplant and cheese, placing the rolls in rows. (Can be made ahead, covered, and refrigerated for up to 8 hours.)

5. Heat oven to 400°F. Bake until rolls are puffed and firm, about 45 minutes.

French Onion Soup Gratinée

For best results, buy sliced Swiss cheese that is long enough to hang over the edges of your soup crocks or mugs. This soup always impresses—no one has to know how easy it actually is.

PREP TIME: 15 MINUTES • COOK TIME: 1¼ HOURS • MAKES: 3 QUARTS (6 TO 8 SERVINGS)

2 tablespoons extra-virgin olive oil
3 pounds yellow onions (6 to 8), sliced
Salt and freshly ground black pepper
2 cups dry white wine
1 quart low-sodium beef broth

For each serving:
1⅔-inch thick diagonal slice of baguette,
2 slices imported Swiss cheese (about ¾ pound total)
2 slices provolone cheese (about ¾ pound total)

1. In a 6-quart saucepot over medium heat, heat oil. Add onions and 1 teaspoon salt. Cook, stirring, 5 minutes. Pour in wine, partially cover, and simmer, stirring occasionally, for 30 minutes. Add broth and 4 cups water and simmer until onions are very tender, about 30 minutes more. Season to taste with salt and pepper.

2. When ready to serve, heat broiler. Place a slice of bread in each ovenproof crock or mug, with an edge protruding above lip of dish. Ladle hot soup over bread. Arrange 4 cheese slices on top of each serving. Broil until cheese is bubbly and golden.

Mashed Potato Soup

Serve this comforting soup with your favorite potato toppers.

PREP TIME: 5 MINUTES • COOK TIME: 15 MINUTES • MAKES: 4 TO 6 SERVINGS

3 cups milk
1½ cups low-sodium chicken broth
3 cups potato flakes
⅓ cup crumbled cooked bacon, for garnish
1 cup sour cream
Salt and freshly ground black pepper
1 cup shredded cheddar cheese, for
  garnish

1. In a large saucepan, whisk together milk, broth, and 1½ cups water. Over medium heat, whisk in potato flakes. Bring to boiling, whisking constantly. Reduce heat to medium-low and simmer, whisking, 5 minutes longer.

2. Place bacon on a paper towel-lined microwave-proof plate and heat on high power until crisp, 1 minute.

3. Remove soup from heat and stir in sour cream. Season to taste with salt and pepper. To serve, ladle into bowls and sprinkle with bacon and cheese. Serve immediately.

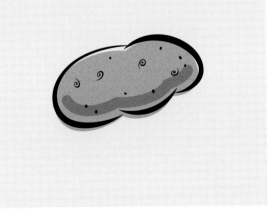

Spring Pea Soup

This refreshing soup marries well with a simple ham and watercress sandwich or toasted Swiss on rye, but if you want to serve the soup alone, add a generous mound of chopped cooked shrimp topped with a dollop of sour cream in the center of each bowl.

PREP TIME: 10 MINUTES • COOK TIME: 20 MINUTES • MAKES: 6 SERVINGS

2 boxes (10 ounces each) frozen baby peas, thawed
2 medium onions, peeled and quartered
2 teaspoon jarred minced garlic
2½ cups low-sodium chicken broth
1 cup milk
Salt and freshly ground black pepper
Pumpernickel croutons, for garnish

1. In a medium saucepan over medium-high heat, combine peas, onions, garlic, and broth. Bring to boiling, reduce heat to medium-low, and simmer until onions are tender, about 15 minutes.

2. Pour a third of the soup into a blender container, cover, and purée. Strain through a fine mesh sieve into a clean saucepan. Repeat twice with remaining soup.

3. Stir in milk and reheat soup over medium heat. Season with salt and pepper. To serve, ladle soup into serving bowls and garnish with croutons.

VARIATION

Broccoli and Cheddar Cheese Soup
Omit the peas and the milk. Substitute 2 boxes (10 ounces each) frozen broccoli pieces, thawed. Continue as directed. Purée warm soup in 3 batches, dividing 8 ounces sharp cheddar, cut into small cubes, among them. Pour purée into clean saucepot (do not strain) and reheat over medium-low heat, stirring, until hot (do not boil). Serve as directed above.

Throw It Into the Oven and Wait

Cornish Hens with Balsamic Mandarin Glaze

This dish is perfect for entertaining. Serve it with Nutty Herbed Rice Pilaf (p. 166) and a green vegetable (I like asparagus).

PREP TIME: 10 MINUTES • COOK TIME: 50 MINUTES • MAKES: 4 SERVINGS

4 Cornish hens (1¼ pounds each)
2 tablespoons balsamic vinegar
1 tablespoon extra-virgin olive oil
1 can (6 ounces) mandarin oranges
Salt and freshly ground black pepper

1. Place rack in upper third of oven and heat oven to 400°F.

2. Arrange hens in a large roasting pan. In a measuring cup, stir together vinegar, oil, and 1 tablespoon juice from mandarin oranges and brush on hens. Season with salt and pepper. Roast until leg joints are loose and an instant-read thermometer inserted in the thickest part of the thigh reads 155°F, about 45 minutes.

3. Transfer hens to a platter. Skim fat from pan juices and stir in orange segments. Season to taste and serve with hens.

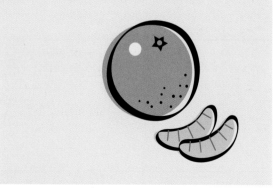

Perfect Roast Chicken

Very few things are as satisfying as a juicy roast chicken with crispy skin. I love it with Creamed Spinach (p. 142) and any kind of potato.

PREP TIME: 5 MINUTES • COOK TIME: 1 HOUR • MAKES: 4 SERVINGS

1 broiler chicken (about 3½ pounds)
1 small apple, cored and cut into quarters
2 tablespoons red wine vinaigrette
½ teaspoon dried thyme
1 tablespoon all-purpose flour
¾ cup low-sodium chicken broth
Salt and freshly ground black pepper

1. Place rack in center of oven and heat to 400°F. Remove bag of giblets from chicken and discard. Wash chicken inside and out and pat dry with paper towels. Place in a shallow roasting pan, insert apple pieces into cavity, and brush with vinaigrette. Sprinkle with thyme.

2. Roast until an instant-read thermometer inserted in the thickest part of the thigh reads 155°F (or until the juices run clear when the thickest part of the thigh is pierced with a fork), 50 to 60 minutes. Transfer chicken to a cutting board with grooves.

3. Pour pan juices into a glass measuring cup and spoon off fat. Using a fork, whisk in flour, then broth. Pour mixture into the roasting pan and bring to boiling over medium-high heat, whisking until thickened, about 3 minutes. Season with salt and pepper. Cut the chicken into pieces and serve with gravy on the side.

VARIATION

Roasted Chicken Pieces
Arrange one chicken cut in eighths on a baking sheet, brush skin with vinaigrette, and sprinkle with thyme. Roast in upper third of oven at 400°F for about 35 minutes. Make gravy as directed above.

Perfect Roast Turkey with Pan Gravy

The secret to a juicy, evenly cooked turkey is to let the bird stand at room temperature (72°F) for an hour before cooking.

PREP TIME: 1¾ HOURS • COOK TIME: 3 HOURS • MAKES: 12 SERVINGS

1 turkey (20 pounds)
1 orange, cut in quarters
1 tablespoon unsalted butter, melted
⅓ cup prepared citrus marinade
¼ teaspoon dried fines herbes
Salt and freshly ground black pepper
½ cup all-purpose flour
3 cups low-sodium chicken broth

1. Remove turkey from refrigerator and let stand at room temperature (70°F or cooler) for 1½ hours.

2. Heat oven to 400°F. Place turkey in a large roasting pan and insert orange quarters into cavity. Brush with melted butter and citrus marinade, and sprinkle with herbs, salt, and pepper. Roast for 2 hours at 400°F. Reduce temperature to 350°F and roast until an instant-read thermometer inserted in the thickest part of the thigh reads 165°F, about 1 hour longer. Transfer turkey to a large platter.

3. Skim fat from pan juices. In a measuring cup, stir together flour and 1 cup broth. Place roasting pan on stove over medium-high heat. Add broth mixture to pan and cook, whisking, until thick. Whisk in remaining broth and bring to boiling, then keep whisking 5 minutes longer. Season to taste with salt and pepper. Carve turkey and serve with gravy.

Stuffed Turkey Meatloaf

For variety, fill the loaf with 2 cups of another favorite frozen or cooked fresh vegetable, such as broccoli or carrots, and different kinds of cheese, such as Cheddar or Swiss.

PREP TIME: 20 MINUTES• BAKE TIME: 1 HOUR 10 MINUTES • MAKES: 6 TO 8 SERVINGS

1 package (10 ounces) sliced mushrooms
2 tablespoons unsalted butter
2 cups frozen chopped onion
2 packages (1⅓ pounds each) ground turkey
2 large eggs
1 cup low-sodium chicken broth
⅔ cup plain dried breadcrumbs
1 box (9 ounces) French-cut green beans, thawed
1 cup (4 ounces) shredded mozzarella cheese
¼ teaspoon each salt and freshly ground black pepper

1. Place mushrooms in the bowl of a food processor, with the steel blade attached and pulse until finely chopped. Transfer to a large nonstick skillet. Add butter, onion, salt, and pepper and cook over medium heat, stirring, until soft and golden, about 6 minutes. Transfer to a bowl and let cool 5 minutes. Add turkey, eggs, broth, and breadcrumbs; mix with hands until blended.

2. On a baking sheet, shape meat into a 9-inch square. Arrange green beans, then cheese down center, leaving a 2-inch border on each of short ends of pan. Fold the long sides over the filling and crimp to seal, leaving a small vent in the top so the loaf doesn't split while baking. Form meat into a 9 x 5-inch loaf.

3. Bake until an instant-read thermometer inserted near the center of the loaf reads 145°F, about 1 hour and 10 minutes.

VARIATION

Spicy Stuffed Meatloaf
Omit the green beans and mozzarella cheese. Substitute 1 cup shredded pepper Jack cheese and 2 cups bell pepper strips. Prepare as directed above.

Mediterranean-Style Turkey Breast

Fold foil in half to create a "tent" for the turkey breast to keep it from drying out.

PREP TIME: 10 MINUTES • COOK TIME: 1¾ HOURS • MAKES: 8 SERVINGS

1 fresh turkey breast (6½ pounds)
1 jar roasted red peppers with garlic in oil, drained and oil reserved
½ teaspoon seasoned salt
Salt and freshly ground black pepper
1 bag (24 ounces) blanched diced potatoes
¼ cup pitted black olives, coarsely chopped

1. Heat oven to 400°F. Place turkey breast in a roasting pan and brush with 2 tablespoons of the reserved pepper oil. Sprinkle with seasoned salt and black pepper and roast for 1 hour.

2. Remove pan from oven. Add potatoes in a single layer to pan and cover turkey loosely with foil tent. Return pan to oven and roast, turning potatoes occasionally, until potatoes are tender and turkey thermometer pops, or until an instant-read thermometer inserted in the thickest part of the thigh reads 155°F, about 45 more minutes. Transfer turkey to a cutting board.

3. Meanwhile, cut peppers into strips. In a skillet over medium heat, warm pepper strips, stirring. Add potatoes and olives and season to taste with salt and pepper. Skim fat from pan juices and discard. Slice turkey and serve with peppers and potatoes and pan juices.

Top Round of Beef Roasted Over Vegetables

As the meat roasts, the vegetables for this dish braise in a robust combination of garlic, tomato, and meat juices. Serve this one-dish wonder with sour cream flavored with prepared horseradish.

PREP TIME: 10 MINUTES • COOK TIME: 1¾ HOURS • MAKES: 6 TO 8 SERVINGS

2 pounds blanched diced potatoes (from 2 24-ounce bags)

2 pounds frozen whole green beans

1 pound yellow onions (3 medium), thinly sliced

1½ pounds tomatoes (5 medium), thinly sliced

3 tablespoons roasted garlic vinaigrette

1 trimmed bottom round beef roast (4½ to 5 pounds)

1. Heat oven to 425°F. In a 3-quart shallow oven-to-table casserole, combine potatoes, green beans, onions, and half of the tomato slices. Add 2 tablespoons vinaigrette, toss well, and then pat vegetables evenly in pan. Top with remaining tomato slices. Bake for 15 minutes.

2. After 15 minutes of cooking, place beef on vegetables, brush remaining vinaigrette on beef, and insert a meat thermometer in thickest part of meat. Roast for 20 minutes, reduce oven temperature to 350°F and continue roasting until internal temperature of meat reaches 125°F for medium-rare, about 1 hour longer. Transfer beef to a cutting board with grooves and let stand 5 minutes. (The temperature will increase as meat rests, cooking the meat a little more.)

3. Thinly slice beef against the grain and arrange on top of vegetables. Pour any juices over meat and vegetables and serve.

Tomato-Braised Brisket

If you like, serve this tasty brisket tossed with fettuccine or other long pasta.

PREP TIME: 5 MINUTES • COOK TIME: 3¼ HOURS • MAKES: 4 SERVINGS

2 pounds beef brisket
Salt and freshly ground black pepper
1 packet (1.4 ounces) onion soup mix
1 tablespoon minced garlic
1 can (28 ounces) crushed tomatoes

1. Place rack in lower third of oven and heat oven to 325°F. Season brisket on both sides with salt and pepper. Over medium heat, heat a 4-quart heavy saucepot. Add brisket and cook until browned on both sides, about 10 minutes, turning once.

2. Add soup mix, garlic, tomatoes, and 2½ cups water to saucepot. Cover and bring to boiling. Transfer saucepot to oven and braise until meat is tender when pierced with a fork, 2½ to 3 hours.

3. Transfer brisket to a cutting board and, using a knife and fork, pull meat into long shreds, then return meat to saucepot. Season to taste with pepper. Serve immediately.

VARIATIONS

Barbecue Braised Brisket
Omit canned tomatoes. Substitute 1 cup low-sodium beef broth, ¾ cup barbecue sauce, and 4¼ cups water. Prepare as directed above.

Slow Brisket Chili
Add 1 cup low-sodium beef broth and 1¼ cups water to the saucepot before braising. After shredding, add a can (15.5 ounces) of your favorite beans, drained and rinsed. Serve over warmed soft corn tortillas and sprinkle with shredded pepper Jack cheese.

My Favorite Meatloaf

You can double this recipe and mix up an extra meatloaf to freeze for another night. To thaw, transfer to the refrigerator the night before. Creamy Dreamy Mashed Potatoes (p. 155) are the perfect comforting side for this classic dish.

PREP TIME: 10 MINUTES • COOK TIME: 50 MINUTES • MAKES: 4 SERVINGS

2 pounds lean ground beef
1 package (1.4 ounces) onion soup mix
⅔ cup plain dried bread crumbs
⅔ cup tomato sauce
2 large eggs

1. Heat oven to 350°F. Grease a 9-inch deep-dish pie pan.

2. In a large bowl, combine beef, soup mix, breadcrumbs, tomato sauce, ⅓ cup water, and eggs. Using your hands, mix until well blended. Transfer to prepared pan and form into a loaf.

3. Bake until firm to the touch, about 50 minutes. Let cool 5 minutes before serving.

Baked Fresh Ham with Garlic Gravy

This big roast can feed a crowd for Christmas, Easter, or any special occasion. If you make it for a group of six, you'll have plenty of leftovers—perfect for making Pulled Pork (p. 66).

PREP TIME: 15 MINUTES • ROAST TIME: 2¼ HOURS • MAKES: 6 TO 12 SERVINGS

1 bone-in fresh ham (about 10 pounds),
    fat trimmed to ¼ inch
½ teaspoon caraway seeds
Salt and freshly ground black pepper
1 cup frozen chopped onion
1 tablespoon jarred minced garlic
1 packet (1 ounce) brown sauce mix
1 tablespoon whole-grain mustard

1. Place rack in lower third of oven and heat to 400°F. Place ham, rounded side up, in a large heavy roasting pan. Sprinkle with caraway seeds and season with salt and pepper. Insert an ovenproof meat thermometer deep into thickest part of ham. Roast 30 minutes.

2. Reduce oven temperature to 350°F, and roast until the internal temperature reaches 155°F, about 1¾ hours longer. Transfer roast to a cutting board with grooves and cover loosely with foil.

3. Pour off all but 2 tablespoons drippings from roasting pan. Place pan over medium heat and add onion and garlic. Cook, stirring, until softened, 3 to 4 minutes. In a small bowl, whisk together sauce mix, mustard, and 2 cups water until smooth. Add mixture to pan and simmer, whisking, until sauce is thickened, 5 to 6 minutes. Season to taste with salt and pepper. To serve, slice ham, place slices on a platter, and serve with gravy on the side.

Glazed Ham with Pineapple and Onions

Serve this for a Sunday dinner with 3-Ingredient Macaroni and Cheese (p. 79) and Portobello and Green Bean Casserole (p. 152).

PREP TIME: 10 MINUTES • COOK TIME: 1 1/2 HOURS • MAKES: 6 SERVINGS

1 fully cooked cured half ham (shank end, about 6 to 7 pounds)

4 large onions, peeled and each cut into 6 wedges

1 can (20 ounces) pineapple chunks, drained, juice reserved

2 tablespoons maple syrup

1 tablespoon whole-grain mustard

1 tablespoon cider vinegar

1. Place rack in lower third of oven and heat oven to 375°F. Place ham in a roasting pan and scatter onions around. Add the reserved pineapple juice to the pan. Cover pan snugly with foil and roast 1 hour.

2. In a measuring cup, stir together maple syrup, mustard, and vinegar. Remove pan from oven and carefully remove foil. Brush ham with maple mixture, add pineapple chunks to pan, and roast, uncovered, 30 minutes longer. Transfer ham to a cutting board. Slice and place on a serving platter along with onions and pineapple.

Cuban-Style Roast Pork

Use the leftovers to make Cuban Heros (p. 108).

PREP TIME: 10 MINUTES • COOK TIME: 45 MINUTES • MAKES: 4 TO 6 SERVINGS

3 tablespoons roasted garlic soup mix
Juice of 1 lemon
1 teaspoon dried oregano, crumbled
1 teaspoon chili powder
⅛ teaspoon freshly ground black pepper
1 boneless pork loin (about 3 pounds)

1. Place rack in center of oven and heat oven to 400°F. Pour soup mix into a small bowl and add lemon juice. Stir in ½ cup water, oregano, chili powder, and pepper.

2. Place pork in a medium roasting pan. Spoon garlic mixture over pork. Roast until an instant-read thermometer inserted in the center of the roast reads 155°F, about 45 minutes. Transfer pork to a cutting board, cover loosely with foil, and let stand 5 minutes before carving.

3. Add ⅔ cup water to roasting pan and stir, scraping up any brown bits from bottom of pan. Slice pork, place on a serving platter, and serve with pan juices.

Mexican Pork Roast

Sofrito is an authentic Spanish cooking sauce made of tomatoes, mild chiles, and garlic and is typically used to flavor beans and stews. Serve this roast with Creamy Cheese Polenta (p. 164).

PREP TIME: 20 MINUTES • **COOK TIME: 45 MINUTES** • **MAKES: 4 SERVINGS**

1 boneless pork loin (about 2¼ pounds)
1 cup sofrito

1. In a large bowl, combine pork and sofrito. Let marinate at room temperature for 15 minutes. (If marinating more than 15 minutes, cover and refrigerate.)

2. Heat oven to 400°F. Transfer pork to a small roasting pan and roast until an instant-read thermometer inserted in the center of the roast reads 155°F, about 45 minutes.

3. Transfer to a cutting board and let stand 5 minutes before carving. To serve, slice into ¼-inch-thick slices and arrange on a serving platter. Serve immediately.

Roasted Pork Loin with Dried Fruit Stuffing

Soy-Roasted Green Beans (p. 151) and packaged couscous alongside will make a great meal.

PREP TIME: 20 MINUTES • COOK TIME: 1¼ HOURS • MAKES: 6 TO 8 SERVINGS

1 boneless pork loin (about 3 pounds)
1½ cups mixed dried fruit (figs, prunes, apricots)
Kitchen twine
2 tablespoons butter, melted
1 teaspoon dried thyme
1 teaspoon minced garlic
Salt and freshly ground black pepper
1 cup low-sodium chicken broth
1 tablespoon molasses

1. Heat oven to 350°F. Cut a lengthwise slash along pork loin without cutting completely through meat, to make a pocket. Stuff dried fruit evenly inside pocket. Use kitchen twine to tie roast closed in several sections. Place in a large roasting pan.

2. In a small bowl, stir together butter, thyme, garlic, and ½ teaspoon each salt and pepper. Brush on pork. In the same bowl, whisk together broth and molasses. Drizzle over pork.

3. Roast pork, basting occasionally, until an instant-read thermometer inserted in center of roast reads 155°F, about 1¼ hours. Transfer roast to a cutting board, let stand 10 minutes, then slice and transfer to a serving platter. Skim fat from pan juices, season to taste with salt and pepper, and serve with pork.

Leg of Lamb with Mediterranean Vegetables

This one-dish meal is especially good to serve on Easter or Passover.

PREP TIME: 10 MINUTES • COOK TIME: 2½ HOURS • MAKES: 6 TO 8 SERVINGS

2 pounds packaged diced red potatoes
1 pound yellow onions (about 3 medium onions), thinly sliced
1 pound eggplant (1 medium), sliced ¼ inch thick
1 cup frozen bell pepper strips
1 can (14 ounces) crushed tomatoes
¼ cup fresh lemon juice
2 tablespoons extra-virgin olive oil
1 tablespoon minced garlic
1½ teaspoons dried oregano
1 teaspoon salt
¼ teaspoon freshly ground black pepper
1 semi-boneless leg of lamb (about 6 pounds)

1. Place a rack in center of oven and heat oven to 425°F. In a 3-quart shallow casserole, combine potatoes, onions, eggplant, bell pepper, and tomatoes. In a measuring cup, stir together lemon juice, oil, garlic, oregano, salt, and pepper. Spoon half the mixture over vegetables; toss well, then press vegetables into an even layer. Roast for 30 minutes.

2. Place lamb on top of vegetables, spoon remaining garlic mixture over lamb and roast 30 minutes. Reduce oven temperature to 350°F and roast until an instant-read thermometer inserted in thickest part of lamb reads 140°F (medium), about 1½ hours longer. Remove pan from oven and reduce oven temperature to 200°F.

3. Transfer lamb to a cutting board and return vegetables to oven. Let lamb stand 10 minutes, then slice lamb thinly, perpendicular to the bone, turning leg as necessary for even slices. Serve with vegetables.

Roasted Veal Loin with Bacon and Crisp Potatoes

If you like, continue the bacon theme and serve Brussels Sprouts with Bacon and Sour Cream (p. 138) alongside.

PREP TIME: 5 MINUTES • COOK TIME: 55 MINUTES • MAKES: 6 SERVINGS

1 ½ tablespoons extra-virgin olive oil
2 pounds wedge-style oven fries
1 teaspoon dried rosemary, crumbled
¾ teaspoon salt
½ teaspoon freshly ground black pepper
1 boneless veal loin roast (about 3 pounds)
3 thick slices smoked bacon

1. Place rack in center of oven and heat oven to 500°F. Lightly grease a large roasting pan with the oil.

2. Place potatoes in prepared pan. Add ½ teaspoon rosemary, ½ teaspoon salt, and ¼ teaspoon pepper. Toss until combined.

3. Sprinkle remaining ½ teaspoon rosemary and remaining salt and pepper on veal. Lay bacon across veal and secure with toothpicks.

4. Place veal in center of pan, arranging potatoes evenly around, and roast 40 minutes. Reduce oven temperature to 400°F and roast until an instant-read thermometer inserted in center of veal reaches 140°F, about 15 minutes longer for medium. Transfer veal to a cutting board and let stand 10 minutes. Thinly slice and serve with potatoes.

Quick, Cool, and Crispy

Spinach-Goat Cheese Pita Pizzas

Substitute baby arugula for the spinach to make a peppery version of these healthy pizzas.

PREP TIME: 10 MINUTES • COOK TIME: 12 MINUTES • MAKES: 4 SERVINGS

4 (6-inch) whole-wheat pita breads
1 jar (12 ounces) roasted red peppers
   with garlic in oil
1 log (10 ounces) fresh goat cheese
Freshly ground black pepper
1 package (5 ounces) baby spinach

1. Heat oven to 500°F. Split each pita to make 2 rounds and place cut-side up on 2 large baking sheets. Remove peppers from oil (reserving oil). Cut peppers into strips and arrange on pitas. Dot pitas with goat cheese and sprinkle with pepper.

2. Bake on bottom rack of oven until cheese is melted and golden and crust is crisp, 10 to 12 minutes. Let cool slightly, then top each pizza with a handful of spinach and drizzle with red pepper oil. Serve immediately.

Pizza à la Baguette

Use leftover Baked Fresh Ham with Garlic Gravy (p. 94) for these tasty baguettes.

PREP TIME: 10 MINUTES • COOK TIME: 10 MINUTES • MAKES: 4 SERVINGS

2½ cups shredded Swiss cheese

½ cup chopped baked or boiled ham
  (about 2 ounces)

⅓ cup mayonnaise

1 (24-inch-long) baguette, split lengthwise

1 can (8 ounces) sliced mushrooms

1 can (14 ounces) artichoke hearts,
  drained and quartered

1. Heat oven to 400°F. In a medium bowl, combine 1 cup Swiss cheese, ham, and mayonnaise. Stir until combined. Spread mixture on cut sides of baguette and place baguette halves on a baking sheet. Cover with mushrooms and artichoke pieces, then sprinkle with remaining cheese.

2. Bake until edges are crisp and cheese is bubbly, about 10 minutes. Remove from oven, cut each piece in half crosswise, and serve immediately.

Mini Pita Pizzas

Serve these quick pizzas with a green salad. Kids love to help make these—feel free to experiment with your favorite toppings.

PREP TIME: 10 MINUTES • **COOK TIME: 10 MINUTES** • **MAKES: 4 SERVINGS**

6 small (4- to 5-inch) whole wheat or
   white pita breads
1 cup tomato pasta sauce or pizza sauce
1 package (3.5 ounces) thinly sliced
   turkey pepperoni
2 small zucchini, thinly sliced
1½ cups shredded mozzarella cheese

1. Heat oven to 500°F. Split each pita to make 2 rounds and place cut-side up on 2 baking sheets. Spread a tablespoon of tomato sauce evenly on each round. Arrange pepperoni and zucchini on each and sprinkle with mozzarella.

2. Bake on bottom rack of oven until cheese is bubbly and golden and crust is crisp, 8 to 10 minutes. Let cool slightly.

Mexican Pizza

These quick little pizzas are perfect slumber-party fare.

PREP TIME: 10 MINUTES • COOK TIME: 20 MINUTES • MAKES: 4 SERVINGS

4 (10-inch) flour tortillas
1 can (15.5 ounces) black beans, drained
   and rinsed
4 cups Mexican-blend shredded cheese
1 medium tomato, diced
Salsa verde and guacamole, for garnish

1. Place oven rack in lower third of oven and heat oven to 450°F.

2. Place 2 flour tortillas on each of 2 large baking sheets. Cover each with ⅓ cup beans and 1 cup cheese, leaving a 1-inch border. Bake until edges of tortillas are browned and cheese is bubbly and golden, about 10 minutes. Repeat with remaining tortillas, beans, and cheese.

3. To serve, cut each pizza into quarters. Sprinkle with diced tomato, and dot each quarter with a teaspoonful each of salsa and guacamole. Serve immediately.

Broccoli Frittata

To add zing to this dish, use ½ cup Pepper Jack cheese in place of half of the cheese blend.

PREP TIME: 5 MINUTES • COOK TIME: 15 MINUTES • MAKES: 4 SERVINGS

1 box (10 ounces) frozen broccoli cuts
2 tablespoons salted butter
6 large eggs
1 cup shredded two-cheese blend
  (cheddar and Monterey Jack)

1. Place broccoli in a small bowl and microwave until thawed, about 3 minutes. Heat oven to 350°F.

2. In an ovenproof medium skillet over medium-high heat, melt butter. Add broccoli and cook, stirring until heated through, about 2 minutes.

3. In a medium bowl, beat together eggs and 3 tablespoons water. Add to skillet and cook, stirring, until halfway scrambled, about 2 minutes. Stir in cheese. Using the back of a spoon, smooth the top. Transfer skillet to oven and bake until moist but firm to the touch, about 10 minutes. To serve, cut into wedges. Serve warm or at room temperature.

VARIATION

Bacon-Potato Frittata
Omit broccoli and cheese blend. Substitute 2 cups blanched diced potatoes, 1 cup shredded Swiss cheese and ½ cup crumbled bacon. Cook potatoes in butter until golden. Add eggs and cook as in step 3 above. Just before baking, stir cheese and bacon into the egg mixture. Bake as directed above .

Chicken and Asparagus Tarts

Cut into eighths, these simple tarts could be a tasty hors d'oeuvre.

PREP TIME: 5 MINUTES • BAKE TIME: 15 MINUTES • MAKES: 4 SERVINGS

2 (10-inch) flour tortillas
3 cups sliced cooked chicken
1 box (9 ounces) frozen asparagus,
    thawed, or 12 cooked asparagus spears
4 ounces goat cheese crumbles
2 tablespoons extra-virgin olive oil

1. Place oven rack in lower third of oven and heat oven to 450°F.

2. Place tortillas on a baking sheet. Arrange chicken on top, leaving a 1-inch border. Top each with half of the asparagus, sprinkle each with half the goat cheese, and drizzle with 1 tablespoon oil.

3. Bake until the edges are lightly browned and cheese is melted and golden, 10 to 15 minutes. Cut each tortilla into quarters and serve warm.

Cuban Heros

In my opinion, there are very few sandwiches that can compete with a Cuban.

PREP TIME: 5 MINUTES • COOK TIME: 10 MINUTES • MAKES: 4 SERVINGS

4 soft (6-inch) sub rolls
¼ cup chipotle mayonnaise
8 slices Swiss cheese
1 pound sliced roast pork or leftover
   Cuban-Style Pork (p. 96)
8 slices boiled ham
8 bread-and-butter pickle sandwich slices
Potato chips and coleslaw, for serving

1. Heat oven to 400°F or heat a sandwich press.

2. Split open sub rolls and spread with mayonnaise. Layer each sandwich with a slice of cheese, a layer of pork, 2 slices of ham, 1 pickle, remaining pork, and a slice of cheese. Close sandwiches and grill or bake until bread is toasted and filling is heated through, about 5 minutes. Serve immediately with potato chips and coleslaw on the side.

Cheese Steak Heros

Use whichever cheese slices you prefer—Swiss, provolone, or cheddar, or a combination.

PREP TIME: 5 MINUTES • COOK TIME: 15 MINUTES • MAKES: 4 SERVINGS

2 tablespoons olive oil
2 medium onions, thinly sliced
8 frozen Philly-style sandwich steaks
8 packaged cheese slices
4 (7-inch) soft sub rolls, split
3 cups washed salad greens
2 tablespoons bottled red wine vinaigrette

1. Heat oven to 200°F. In a 12-inch nonstick skillet over medium heat, heat oil. Add onions and cook, stirring, 3 minutes. Add ¼ cup water and cook until onions are soft and golden, 2 minutes longer. Transfer to a bowl.

2. Add 2 steaks to the same pan, cook 1 minute, flip, then cover each with 1 slice of cheese. Stack slices, transfer to a roll, and cover with one-fourth of the onions. Place on a baking sheet and transfer to the oven to keep warm. Repeat with remaining steaks, cheese slices, and rolls.

3. In a medium bowl, toss greens with vinaigrette. Divide greens evenly among sandwiches and serve immediately.

Sausage and Pepper Subs

Be sure to have plenty of napkins on hand while you're eating these delicious (but messy!) subs.

PREP TIME: 5 MINUTES • COOK TIME: 18 MINUTES • MAKES: 4 SERVINGS

1½ packages (1 pound each) sweet Italian sausage, removed from casings
2 cups shredded mozzarella cheese
1 bag (1 pound) frozen onions and pepper strips
2 cups tomato-basil pasta sauce
4 (7-inch) soft sub rolls, split

1. Heat oven to 400°F. Place sub rolls on a baking sheet.

2. Heat a 12-inch nonstick skillet over medium heat. Shape sausage into four 7-inch oblong patties about ⅓ inch thick. Place in skillet and cook, turning once, until browned and just cooked through, about 7 minutes. Transfer patties to rolls and cover each with ½ cup cheese.

3. Increase heat to high. Add and onions to skillet and cook, stirring, until liquid has evaporated, about 6 minutes. Stir in pasta sauce. Divide mixture among sandwiches.

4. Bake sandwiches until rolls are toasted, 4 to 5 minutes. Serve hot.

VARIATION

Meatball and Pepper Subs
Omit Italian sausage. Substitute one package (15 ounces) frozen cooked meatballs, thawed and sliced in half. In a 12-inch nonstick skillet over medium heat, warm meatballs in pasta sauce just until heated through, about 5 minutes. Transfer to sub rolls and continue as directed above.

Sloppy Janes

These are sloppy Joes with a Southern twist. Use Seedy Slaw (p. 162), instead of prepared, if you prefer.

PREP TIME: 5 MINUTES   •   **COOK TIME: 10 MINUTES**   •   **MAKES: 4 SERVINGS**

1¼ pounds lean ground beef
1 cup frozen chopped onion and green bell
   pepper
¾ cup barbecue sauce
Salt and freshly ground black pepper
4 hamburger buns
1 pound coleslaw

1. In a nonstick medium skillet over medium-high heat, brown ground beef with onion and green pepper, using a wooden spoon to break up meat, about 5 minutes.

2. Add barbecue sauce, reduce heat to medium, and stir until heated through, about 4 minutes. Season to taste with salt and pepper.

3. To serve, split buns and place on plates. Spoon mixture onto bottom halves of buns, spoon coleslaw over, and cover with top halves of buns. Serve immediately.

Potato Chip Tuna Melts

You can make these in a sandwich press or in the toaster oven. Use sandwich slices of Swiss in place of the cheddar if you like. Serve these with tomato soup for a hearty meal on a cool evening.

PREP TIME: 10 MINUTES • COOK TIME: 10 MINUTES • MAKES: 4 SERVINGS

1 can (12 ounces) solid white tuna in oil, drained
2 celery ribs, finely chopped
¼ cup mayonnaise
½ tablespoon white wine vinegar
8 slices marble rye bread
12 sandwich slices cheddar cheese
1 large tomato, sliced into 8 slices
2 cups slightly crushed potato chips

1. Heat a sandwich press, if using.

2. Using a fork, flake the tuna into a medium bowl. Add celery, mayonnaise, and vinegar and stir well.

3. Lay 4 slices of bread on work surface. Cover each with 1 slice of cheese, 2 tomato slices, and another slice of cheese. Mound tuna on top of each portion, top with 1 more slice of cheese and another slice of bread. Grill in a press or toast 2 sandwiches at a time in toaster oven set on medium-dark until bread is toasted and cheese is melted.

4. Open sandwiches, top tuna with potato chips, close, and cut in half. Serve hot.

Portobello Melt

In summer, cook the mushrooms outside on a charcoal grill for even better grilled flavor. Toast the buns in a toaster oven if you like.

PREP TIME: 5 MINUTES • COOK TIME: 10 MINUTES • MAKES: 4 SERVINGS

4 medium portobello mushroom caps

$\frac{1}{3}$ cup bottled Caesar dressing

1 package (4 ounces) thinly sliced prosciutto

4 slices provolone cheese

4 hamburger buns or soft round rolls, split

4 large tomato slices

2 cups packaged baby arugula

1. Heat a grill pan over medium heat until hot but not smoking. Meanwhile, brush mushroom caps with dressing. Add mushrooms, top-side up, cover, and cook 4 minutes. Turn, fill each with one-fourth of the prosciutto and cover prosciutto with a slice of provolone. Cover and cook until mushrooms are tender and cheese is melted, about 4 minutes longer.

2. To serve, place buns on each of 4 plates. Place one mushroom on each bottom bun and cover each with a tomato slice and $\frac{1}{2}$ cup arugula. Cover with top halves of buns and serve.

Zucchini, Roasted Pepper, and Cheese Pockets

These veggie-filled pockets are perfect for an after-school snack.

PREP TIME: 15 MINUTES • **BAKE TIME: 10 MINUTES** • **MAKES: 4 SERVINGS**

1 jar (12 ounces) roasted red peppers
   with garlic in olive oil
2 packages (1 pound each) frozen sliced
   zucchini, thawed and patted dry
½ cup frozen chopped onion
4 (10-inch) flour tortillas
1 package (6 to 9 ounces) shredded
   mozzarella cheese

1. Drain red peppers, reserving oil. Slice peppers into 1-inch-wide strips and reserve.

2. In a nonstick 12-inch skillet over medium heat, heat 2 tablespoons reserved pepper oil. Add zucchini and onion and cook, stirring, until tender and golden, about 5 minutes. Stir in roasted peppers.

3. Lay a tortilla on a work surface. Arrange one-fourth of the vegetables down the center (in a 6- x 2-inch mound). Sprinkle with one-fourth of the cheese. Fold in ends over short sides of vegetables, then fold one edge over long side of vegetables and roll up. Repeat with remaining tortillas and vegetables.

4. In toaster oven on medium setting, bake tortilla pockets 2 at a time until golden and crisp. Repeat with remaining pockets. To serve, cut each pocket in half crosswise. Serve hot.

Mu Shu Pork

Add some frozen egg rolls and instant rice: instant Chinese feast!

PREP TIME: 15 MINUTES • **COOK TIME: 10 MINUTES** • **MAKES: 4 SERVINGS**

8 (6-inch) flour tortillas
½ pound boneless pork loin, sliced ¼ inch
    thick and cut into 1-inch strips
2½ tablespoons stir-fry sauce
2 tablespoons vegetable oil
1 can (8 ounces) sliced mushrooms,
    drained
1 bag (1 pound) shredded cabbage
2 carrots, shredded
4 scallions, thinly sliced

1. Heat the oven to 400°F. Wrap tortillas in foil and place in oven to warm.

2. Meanwhile, in a medium bowl, stir together pork and stir-fry sauce. In a nonstick 12-inch skillet over medium high heat, heat 1 tablespoon oil. Add pork to skillet and stir-fry until no longer pink, 2 to 3 minutes. Transfer to a plate.

3. Add remaining oil to skillet. Add mushrooms, cabbage, carrots, and scallions and stir-fry until wilted, about 3 minutes. Return pork and any juices that have collected to skillet and stir-fry to blend flavors, 2 minutes.

4. To serve, divide pork mixture evenly among warmed tortillas and roll loosely. Serve immediately.

Dinner Nachos

No one will be disappointed when you serve these tasty nachos for dinner.

PREP TIME: 5 MINUTES • COOK TIME: 15 MINUTES • MAKES: 6 SERVINGS

1 bag (8 ounces) unsalted tortilla chips
Vegetable-oil cooking spray
3 cups (12 ounces) shredded Mexican-blend cheese
1 pound lean ground beef or ground turkey
1 packet (1.25 ounces) taco seasoning
1 can (15.5 ounces) kidney beans, rinsed and drained
½ cup chopped scallions (green parts only)
Salsa, sour cream, and guacamole, for serving

1. Heat the oven to 350°F. Line 2 baking sheets with foil and spray with cooking spray. Spread chips on prepared baking sheets, sprinkle with cheese, and bake until cheese is just melted, about 8 minutes. Turn off oven.

2. Meanwhile, in a nonstick 12-inch skillet over medium-high heat, cook beef, using a wooden spoon to break it up, until browned, about 4 minutes. Add seasoning and beans and cook, stirring, 2 minutes.

3. Remove chips from oven, transfer with a spatula to a large serving platter, and spoon beef and beans over. Sprinkle with scallions and serve immediately with salsa, sour cream, and guacamole on the side.

Beefy Burritos

Serve these burritos with a simple green salad.

PREP TIME: 10 MINUTES • COOK TIME: 10 MINUTES • MAKES: 4 SERVINGS

8 (6-inch) flour tortillas
¾ pound lean ground beef
1½ tablespoons taco seasoning
1 can (15.5 ounces) small red beans,
   drained and rinsed
1 box (10 ounces) frozen corn, thawed
1 cup medium-hot salsa
1 cup cooked white rice
1 cup shredded cheddar cheese

1. Heat oven to 400°F. Wrap tortillas in foil and place in oven to warm.

2. In a nonstick 12-inch skillet over medium-high heat, combine beef and taco seasoning and cook, using a wooden spoon to break up meat, until browned, about 5 minutes.

3. Add beans, corn, salsa, and rice. Cook, stirring, until heated through, about 3 minutes.

4. Lay 2 warmed tortillas on a work surface. Spoon beef mixture onto tortillas and sprinkle with cheese. Fold in bottom edge (to keep filling from spilling out as you eat) and then roll up. Repeat with remaining tortillas and filling. Serve warm.

Pepper and Egg Sandwiches

A spinach salad pairs perfectly with these savory sandwiches.

PREP TIME: 5 MINUTES • COOK TIME: 10 MINUTES • MAKES: 4 SERVINGS

2 tablespoons olive oil
1 bag (1 pound) frozen onions and pepper strips
8 eggs
¼ teaspoon salt
½ teaspoon freshly ground black pepper.
1 ½ cups shredded mozzarella cheese
4 (7-inch) soft sub rolls, split
1 cup tomato-basil pasta sauce, warmed

1. In a 12-inch nonstick skillet over medium-high heat, combine oil, onions, and peppers, and cook, stirring, until liquid is evaporated and vegetables are tender, about 6 minutes. Reduce heat to medium.

2. In a medium bowl, beat together eggs, ¼ cup water, salt, and pepper. Add to pan and cook, stirring, until halfway scrambled, 2 to 3 minutes. Reduce heat to low. Using the back of a spoon, smooth top of mixture in pan then sprinkle with 1 cup cheese. Cook until the bottom is set, about 1 minute. Fold in half and sprinkle with remaining cheese.

3. Place sub rolls on plates. Cut omelet into 4 portions and transfer to rolls. Spoon tomato sauce over and serve immediately.

Cozy Dogs

These wraps take Pigs in Blankets to a new level, and kids of any age love to help in the preparation. For bigger hot dogs, you'll need twice the dough.

PREP TIME: 10 MINUTES • COOK TIME: 10 MINUTES • MAKES: 4 SERVINGS

1 pound refrigerated pizza dough or bread
   dough
8 (5-inch) turkey hot dogs
8 slices cheddar or Swiss cheese
2 tablespoons olive oil
Mustard and ketchup, for serving

1. Place oven rack in lower third of oven and heat oven to 500°F.

2. Divide dough into 8 equal pieces. Place 1 piece on a work surface and roll out to a 6- x 3-inch rectangle. Wrap a cheese slice around a hot dog, place on bottom edge of dough, and roll tightly, pinching ends to seal. Brush with oil and place seam-side down on a baking sheet. Repeat with remaining dough, hot dogs, and cheese.

3. Bake until browned, about 10 minutes. Let cool 5 minutes before serving. Serve hot with mustard and ketchup on the side.

Chicken and Cheese Quesadillas

These are great for a busy week-night dinner or a casual weekend meal or snack. Serve with a green salad.

PREP TIME: 10 MINUTES • COOK TIME: 15 MINUTES • MAKES: 4 SERVINGS

1 box (10 ounces) frozen leaf spinach, thawed and squeezed dry
1 cup bagged shredded cheddar or Mexican-blend cheese
¼ cup chili powder
8 (8-inch) flour tortillas
1½ cups sliced cooked chicken (8 ounces)
Vegetable-oil cooking spray
Salsa, for serving

1. Heat spinach in the microwave until heated through, about 2 minutes.

2. Meanwhile, in a small bowl, toss together cheese and chili powder until combined.

3. Lay 4 tortillas on a work surface. Top each with one-fourth each chicken, spinach, and cheese. Cover with remaining tortillas.

4. Spray a large skillet with cooking spray and heat over medium heat. Place a quesadilla in the skillet and cook until the bottom is golden, 2 to 3 minutes. Turn carefully with a spatula and cook until golden on other side and filling is heated through, 2 to 3 minutes more. Repeat with remaining quesadillas. Serve immediately with salsa on the side.

VARIATION

Bean and Cheese Quesadillas
Omit chicken. In a small saucepan over medium heat, warm 1 can refried beans. Spread each tortilla evenly with one-fourth of the beans and cook as directed above.

Huevos Rancheros

Breakfast for dinner is always fun. Serve warmed tortilla chips on the side.

PREP TIME: 5 MINUTES • **COOK TIME: 15 MINUTES** • **MAKES: 4 SERVINGS**

2 cans (15 ounces each) low-fat refried
  beans
3 tablespoons safflower oil
8 fresh corn tortillas
8 large eggs
1 1/3 cups shredded cheddar cheese
Salsa, for serving

1. Heat oven to 350°F. Line a baking sheet with foil and set aside.

2. In a covered medium saucepan over medium-low heat, warm refried beans, stirring occasionally.

3. Meanwhile, in a nonstick 12-inch skillet over medium heat, heat 1/2 tablespoon oil. Add 2 tortillas and cook 1 minute per side. Transfer to prepared baking sheet. Spread 1/3 cup warm beans over each tortilla and transfer to oven to keep warm. Repeat with remaining tortillas and beans.

4. Add remaining tablespoon oil to the skillet. Add 4 eggs to the skillet, sprinkle with 1/2 cup cheese, cover, and cook until desired doneness. Transfer tortillas to plates. Cover each with an egg. Repeat with remaining eggs and cheese. Serve with salsa on the side.

Breakfast-for-Dinner Burritos

These would be great as breakfast burritos too.

PREP TIME: 10 MINUTES • COOK TIME: 10 MINUTES • MAKES: 4 SERVINGS

8 (6-inch) flour tortillas

8 large eggs

1 can (4 ounces) chopped green chilies

3 tablespoons salsa

1 tablespoon vegetable oil

1½ cups (6 ounces) shredded Mexican blend cheese, for serving

½ cup chopped scallions (light green parts), for serving

1. Stack tortillas and wrap in foil. Place in oven and heat oven to 350°F. Let tortillas warm for at least 5 minutes.

2. In a medium bowl, beat together eggs, chilies, and salsa. In a nonstick skillet over medium-high heat, heat oil. Add egg mixture and cook, stirring, until scrambled. Transfer eggs to a serving platter.

3. Unwrap warmed tortillas and place 2 on each plate. Top each tortilla with a spoonful of eggs and serve immediately with cheese and scallions on the side.

Greens, Eggs, and Ham

Serve with toasted thick-sliced sourdough from the supermarket bakery.

PREP TIME: 10 MINUTES • COOK TIME: 20 MINUTES • MAKES: 4 SERVINGS

1 tablespoon unsalted butter
¾ cup finely diced baked ham
⅔ cup frozen chopped onion
4 ounces cream cheese
½ cup milk
2 packages (1 pound each) frozen chopped
   spinach, thawed and squeezed dry
Freshly ground black pepper
8 eggs

1. Heat oven to 500°F. In a heavy ovenproof skillet over medium heat, melt butter. Add ham and onion and cook, stirring occasionally, until onion is golden, about 4 minutes. Add cream cheese and milk and stir until smooth. Stir in spinach and cook until heated through, about 4 minutes. Season with pepper.

2. Smooth spinach mixture out into an even layer. Crack eggs over spinach mixture, transfer to oven, and bake until eggs are set but yolks are still runny, about 10 minutes.

VARIATION

Eggs Florentine
Prepare spinach mixture as directed above. Divide the spinach mixture among 4 individual shallow baking dishes. Crack 2 eggs over each and and bake as directed above. Meanwhile, prepare 1 package hollandaise sauce according to package directions. To serve, place each hot dish on a plate and spoon hollandaise sauce over each.

Sausage and Broccoli Baked Potatoes

These potatoes are a filling all-in-one meal.

PREP TIME: 10 MINUTES • **COOK TIME: 30 MINUTES** • **MAKES: 4 SERVINGS**

4 large (8 ounces each) baking potatoes, scrubbed and pierced with a fork
1 box (10 ounces) frozen cut broccoli, thawed
8 fully cooked sausage links, sliced
½ cup (4 ounces) cream cheese
1 cup (4 ounces) shredded cheddar cheese

1. Place oven rack in top third of oven. Heat oven to 450°F.

2. Cook potatoes in microwave at high power for 15 minutes.

3. Meanwhile, in a nonstick medium skillet over medium heat, cook broccoli and sausage until sausage is browned, about 4 minutes. Stir in cream cheese, and heat, stirring, until melted. Stir in cheddar and remove pan from the heat.

4. Place potatoes on a large baking sheet. Cut a slit in each and press ends to split open. Using a fork, flake the inside of potato slightly. Spoon filling into each potato and bake until filling is golden and bubbly, about 10 minutes.

Shrimp and Spinach Baked Potatoes

You might be surprised by the combination of shrimp and potatoes, but try them—you'll be pleasantly surprised.

PREP TIME: 5 MINUTES • COOK TIME: 25 MINUTES • MAKES: 4 SERVINGS

4 large (8 ounces) baking potatoes, scrubbed and pierced with a fork
1 can (4 ounces) tiny shrimp, drained
⅓ cup mayonnaise
⅓ cup sour cream
1 box (10 ounces) frozen chopped spinach, thawed and squeezed dry
1 cup (4 ounces) shredded Monterey Jack or Swiss cheese

1. Place oven rack in top third of oven. Heat oven to 450°F.

2. Cook potatoes in microwave at high power for 15 minutes.

3. Meanwhile, in a medium bowl, stir together shrimp, mayonnaise, sour cream, spinach, and cheese.

4. Place potatoes on a large baking sheet. Cut a slit in each and press ends to split open. Using a fork, flake the inside of the potato slightly. Spoon a generous ⅓ cup filling into each potato and bake until filling is golden and bubbly, about 10 minutes.

Warm Steak, Goat Cheese and Arugula Salad

This elegant salad is a lovely entrée for a summer dinner party.

PREP TIME: 10 MINUTES • COOK TIME: 12 MINUTES • MAKES: 4 SERVINGS

1½ pounds trimmed flank steak
½ teaspoon salt-free lemon pepper
Salt
1 package (10 ounces) baby arugula
⅓ cup sun-dried tomatoes packed in olive
   oil, drained and sliced
¼ cup bottled red wine vinaigrette
1 log (4 or 5 ounces) fresh goat cheese,
   crumbled

1. Heat broiler. Sprinkle both sides of steak with lemon pepper and ¾ teaspoon salt. Broil steak about 4 inches from the heat, turning once, about 12 minutes total for medium-rare. Transfer to a cutting board, cover loosely with foil, and let stand 5 minutes.

2. Meanwhile, in a medium bowl, toss together arugula, sun-dried tomatoes, and dressing. Divide salad among 4 dinner plates. Slice steak as thin as possible, diagonally against the grain. Top salads with sliced steak and sprinkle with goat cheese.

Warm Tuna and White Beans with Sage

Serve this warm salad with Quick 'n' Easy Parmesan Muffins (p. 168) or garlic bread.

PREP TIME: 5 MINUTES • COOK TIME: 13 MINUTES • MAKES: 4 SERVINGS

1 tablespoon extra-virgin olive oil
½ cup frozen chopped onion
1 teaspoon jarred minced garlic
2 cans (15.5 ounces each) cannellini beans, drained and rinsed
½ teaspoon dried sage
2 cans (6 ounces each) tuna in olive oil, drained
Freshly ground black pepper
12 Boston lettuce leaves or radicchio leaves (or a combination), washed and patted dry, for serving

1. In a heavy medium saucepan over medium heat, combine oil, onion, and garlic. Cook, stirring, until fragrant and golden, 4 to 5 minutes. Add beans and sage and cook, stirring, until heated through, 5 to 6 minutes. Stir in tuna and cook until heated through, about 2 minutes. Season to taste with pepper.

2. Arrange 3 lettuce leaves on each of 4 plates. Spoon bean mixture on top and serve immediately.

Quick Chicken Caesar

This is a great way to use a rotisserie chicken from the supermarket. Substitute bottled red wine vinaigrette for the garlic dressing if you prefer.

PREP TIME: 5 MINUTES • MAKES: 4 SERVINGS

½ cup bottled roasted garlic salad
   dressing
1 teaspoon Dijon mustard
1 teaspoon Worcestershire sauce
2 cups shredded cooked chicken
2 packages (6 ounces each) Italian-style
   salad greens
Freshly ground black pepper
¼ cup grated Parmesan cheese
6 Parmesan cheese straws, broken into
   bite-sized pieces

In a large salad bowl, whisk together salad dressing, mustard, and Worcestershire. Add chicken and salad greens and toss well. Season with pepper, sprinkle cheese and cheese straw pieces on top, and toss again. Serve immediately.

Cobb Salad

Serve with your favorite salad dressing (I like blue cheese).

PREP TIME: 15 MINUTES • COOK TIME: 15 MINUTES • MAKES: 4 SERVINGS

4 eggs
8 strips cooked bacon
1 package (10 ounces) salad greens
2 carrots, coarsely grated
3 cups packaged sliced cooked chicken
  (12 ounces)
1 cup (4 ounces) shredded cheddar
  cheese
⅓ cup sliced black olives
½ cup frozen guacamole, thawed
Bottled salad dressing, for serving

1. Place eggs in a small saucepan with water to cover, bring to boiling over high heat, reduce heat, and simmer 10 minutes. Drain eggs, then add ice water to pot to chill eggs.

2. Warm bacon according to microwave instructions on package and tear into pieces.

3. Toss greens and carrots in large salad bowl. Arrange chicken on top, then sprinkle with cheddar cheese, olives, and bacon. Dot with guacamole. Peel and slice eggs and arrange on top. Serve with dressing on the side.

Salad Niçoise

If you have any leftover cooked potatoes, add them to the salad.

PREP TIME: 5 MINUTES • **COOK TIME: 10 MINUTES** • **MAKES: 4 SERVINGS.**

4 large eggs
2 cans (6 ounces each) tuna packed in
   olive oil, drained
1 box (10 ounces) French-cut green
   beans, thawed and drained
1 jar (12 ounces) roasted red peppers
   with garlic in olive oil
1 package mixed baby salad greens
1 ½ tablespoons red wine vinegar
Salt and freshly ground black pepper
⅓ cup black olives, preferably Niçoise, for
   garnish

1. Place eggs in a small saucepan with water to cover, bring to a boil over high heat, reduce heat to low and simmer 10 minutes. Drain eggs and cover with ice water. Set aside.

2. Using a fork, flake tuna into a large bowl and add green beans. Slice enough red pepper to equal ½ cup and add to bowl along with salad greens. Drizzle mixture with vinegar and 3 tablespoons red pepper oil and toss. Season to taste with salt and pepper and divide among 4 plates.

3. Peel eggs, cut each into 4 wedges, and place 4 wedges on each plate. Garnish salads with olives and serve immediately.

1-2-3 Grilled Chicken Salad

Feel free to substitute your favorite vinaigrette. Serve this pretty salad with slices of crusty bread or packaged grissini, which are thin Italian breadsticks.

PREP TIME: 10 MINUTES • COOK TIME: 10 MINUTES • MAKES: 4 SERVINGS

4 large skinless boneless chicken breast
   halves (about 6 ounces each), trimmed
   of fat
¾ cup bottled Vidalia onion-mustard
   vinaigrette or your favorite vinaigrette
Vegetable oil cooking spray
1 package (10 ounces) baby greens
1 cup grape tomatoes, cut in half
Salt and freshly ground black pepper

1. In a medium bowl, combine chicken breasts and ½ cup dressing. Toss until chicken is coated.

2. Heat a nonstick grill pan over medium heat until hot. Spray with cooking spray and add chicken. Cover pan with foil and cook, turning once, until chicken is just cooked through, about 8 minutes total. Transfer chicken to a cutting board and thinly slice crosswise.

3. In a medium bowl, combine remaining ¼ cup dressing, greens, and tomatoes. Add sliced chicken and toss well. Season to taste with salt and pepper and toss again. Serve immediately.

Spinach Salad with Warm Bacon Dressing

Use baby spinach for this classic salad if you prefer.

PREP TIME: 10 MINUTES • COOK TIME: 10 MINUTES • MAKES: 4 SERVINGS

1 package (10 ounces) fresh spinach, torn
   into bite-sized pieces
1 large carrot, grated
½ cup blue cheese crumbles (optional)
1 tablespoon olive oil
1 package (8 ounces) sliced fresh
   mushrooms
½ cup crumbled bacon
⅓ cup bottled red wine vinaigrette
Freshly ground black pepper

1. In a large salad bowl, combine spinach, carrot, and cheese. Set aside.

2. In a nonstick skillet over medium-high heat, heat oil. Add mushrooms and cook, stirring, until softened and browned, about 4 minutes. Stir in bacon and cook 2 minutes. Remove pan from the heat, add vinaigrette, and stir until just heated through.

3. Drizzle dressing over salad, season with pepper, and toss well. Serve immediately.

QUICK, COOL, AND CRISPY

Seven Layer Salad

If you have a clear salad bowl with straight sides, use it to show off the colorful layers of this salad, which is great to take along to a party. Serve it with your favorite dressing on the side.

PREP TIME: 10 MINUTES • COOK TIME: 20 MINUTES • MAKES: 4 SERVINGS

6 large eggs
12 slices cooked bacon
2 medium tomatoes, diced
1 box (10 ounces) frozen peas
1 package (8 ounces) sliced fresh
   mushrooms
1 package (10 ounces) romaine, torn in
   bite-sized pieces
1 ½ cups (6 ounces) shredded cheddar
   cheese
Bottled salad dressing, for serving

1. Place eggs in a small saucepan with water to cover, bring to a boil over high heat, reduce heat to low and simmer 10 minutes. Drain eggs and cover with ice water. Set aside.

2. Meanwhile, microwave bacon according to package directions until crisp. Crumble into 1-inch pieces.

3. In a large serving bowl, layer tomatoes, peas, mushrooms, romaine, cheddar and bacon. Just before serving, cut eggs into quarters and arrange on top. Serve with dressing on the side.

Tuna Waldorf Salad

Serve smaller portions for a first course salad for six or eight.

PREP TIME: 10 MINUTES • COOK TIME: 8 MINUTES • MAKES: 4 SERVINGS

½ cup walnuts
3 cans (6 ounces each) tuna in olive oil,
    drained
2 large celery ribs, thinly sliced
4 scallions, thinly sliced
1 Gala apple, thinly sliced
¾ cup bottled coleslaw dressing
1 package (6 ounces) salad greens

1. Heat the oven to 350°F. Place walnuts on a small baking sheet and toast until slightly fragrant, about 8 minutes. Transfer to a cutting board and chop coarsely. Transfer to a large salad bowl.

2. Add tuna to walnuts, using a fork to flake tuna lightly. Add celery, scallions, apple, and dressing and toss well.

3. Divide salad greens among 4 plates. Mound tuna salad on greens and serve.

Avocado with Shrimp Salad

The easiest way to shell an avocado is to run a spoon between the flesh and the shell. The flesh will come out in one piece.

PREP TIME: 10 MINUTES • MAKES: 4 SERVINGS

1 pound cleaned cooked medium shrimp,
   coarsely chopped
1 large celery rib, finely chopped
1 scallion, finely chopped
2 tablespoons fresh lemon juice
½ cup mayonnaise
Salt and freshly ground black pepper
Lettuce, for serving
1 large tomato, sliced, for serving
2 ripe Hass avocados

1. In a medium bowl, toss together shrimp, celery, scallion, and lemon juice. Add mayonnaise and stir until blended. Season to taste with salt and pepper.

2. Arrange lettuce and tomato slices on each of four salad plates. Cut each avocado in half and remove pits. Remove flesh from the shells and place each half on a plate. Mound shrimp salad on top of each avocado and serve immediately.

Tomatoes Stuffed with Crab Salad

A staple in fifties entertaining, this classic salad never goes out of style.

PREP TIME: 10 MINUTES • MAKES: 4 SERVINGS

1 can (6 ounces) crabmeat, drained
2 celery ribs, finely chopped
¼ cup plus 2 tablespoons mayonnaise
2 tablespoons ketchup
2 teaspoons prepared horseradish
Freshly ground black pepper
1 package (6 ounces) romaine hearts, cut
    crosswise into ¼-inch strips
4 medium tomatoes, cored

1. In a medium bowl combine crabmeat, celery, mayonnaise, ketchup, and horse-radish. Season to taste with pepper and stir until mixed.

2. Divide lettuce among 4 plates. Cut each tomato into 6 wedges, leaving bottoms intact so that wedges stay together. Place a tomato on lettuce, then spoon crab salad into tomatoes. Serve immediately.

Sensational
Sides

Sautéed Brussels Sprouts with Bacon and Sour Cream

This rich dish is a perfect side for Perfect Roast Chicken (p. 87) on a cold evening.

PREP TIME: 5 MINUTES • COOK TIME: 8 MINUTES • MAKES: 6 TO 8 SERVINGS

2 boxes (10 ounces each) frozen Brussels
   sprouts, thawed and halved
½ cup frozen chopped onion
1 tablespoon vegetable oil
⅓ cup bacon crumbles
1 tablespoon cider vinegar
½ cup sour cream
Salt and freshly ground black pepper

1. In a nonstick skillet over medium heat, combine sprouts, onion, oil, and ½ cup water. Cook until water evaporates, about 5 minutes.

2. Add bacon to pan and cook, stirring, until bacon is crisp and sprouts are beginning to brown, about 3 minutes. Stir in vinegar, remove from the heat, and stir in sour cream. Season to taste with salt and pepper.

Glazed Carrots

This is an ideal side dish for Perfect Roast Turkey with Pan Gravy (p. 88).

PREP TIME: 5 MINUTES • COOK TIME: 10 MINUTES • MAKES: 4 SERVINGS

1 bag (8 ounces) fresh baby carrots
2 tablespoons butter
1 tablespoon light brown sugar
Salt and freshly ground black pepper

1. In a medium saucepan over medium heat, combine carrots, butter, sugar, and $\frac{1}{4}$ teaspoon salt.

2. Add 1 cup water, cover, and cook for 5 minutes. Uncover and cook, stirring occasionally, until carrots are tender and glazed, 2 to 3 minutes.

VARIATION

Cinnamon-Glazed Carrots
Add $\frac{1}{4}$ teaspoon ground cinnamon to the sugar. Continue as directed above.

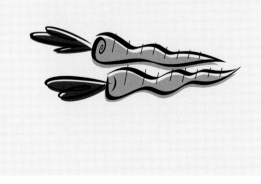

Roasted Broccoli with Garlic

Many people think of broccoli only as steamed or in stir-fries. But roasting brings out a depth of flavor that other cooking methods don't. Serve with Oven-Roasted Filet Mignon (p. 26).

PREP TIME: 5 MINUTES • COOK TIME: 15 MINUTES • MAKES: 6 SERVINGS

3 bags (8 ounces each) fresh broccoli
   florets
2 tablespoons extra-virgin olive oil
2 peeled large garlic cloves, lightly
   crushed
¼ teaspoon red pepper flakes (optional)
¼ teaspoon salt

1. Place rack in upper third of oven and heat oven to 500°F. Line a baking sheet with foil.

2. Rinse broccoli, but do not pat dry. Transfer broccoli to prepared pan. Drizzle with oil; add garlic, pepper flakes, and salt. Toss until broccoli is coated, then arrange on prepared pan in an even layer.

3. Roast in oven until tender and beginning to brown, 10 to 15 minutes. Transfer to a bowl.

Roasted Cauliflower with Cheddar

Even kids love this vegetable! Serve it alongside Baked Fresh Ham with Garlic Gravy (p. 94).

PREP TIME: 10 MINUTES • COOK TIME: 15 MINUTES • MAKES: 6 SERVINGS

1 head fresh cauliflower, cut into small
   florets
1 tablespoon vegetable oil
¼ cup frozen chopped onion
Salt and freshly ground black pepper
1 cup shredded cheddar cheese

1. Place rack in upper third of oven and heat oven to 500°F. Line a baking sheet with foil.

2. Rinse cauliflower; do not pat dry. Transfer florets to prepared pan; drizzle with oil, add onion and ⅛ teaspoon each salt and pepper. Toss well, then spread in an even layer.

3. Roast in oven until tender and beginning to brown, 10 to 15 minutes. To serve, sprinkle cheese on hot cauliflower and transfer to a bowl.

Creamed Spinach

Thaw spinach in microwave or in a colander under cool running water.

PREP TIME: 5 MINUTES • COOK TIME: 10 MINUTES • MAKES: 4 SERVINGS

2 tablespoons butter
½ cup frozen chopped onion
2 boxes (10 ounces each) frozen leaf
   spinach, thawed and squeezed dry
1 cup heavy cream
Salt and freshly ground black pepper

1. In a medium skillet over medium heat, melt the butter. Add onion and cook, stirring occasionally, until golden, about 5 minutes.

2. Add spinach and cream. Bring to a boil over high heat, reduce heat to medium, and cook, stirring, until cream is reduced by half, about 5 minutes. Season to taste with salt and pepper.

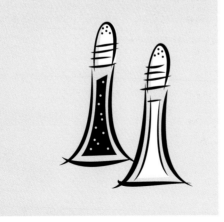

Indian Sautéed Greens

You can use any wilted fresh greens in this preparation, but frozen spinach works nicely and you can always keep it on hand.

PREP TIME: 5 MINUTES • COOK TIME: 10 MINUTES • MAKES: 4 SERVINGS

3 tablespoons vegetable oil
½ cup frozen chopped onion
1 teaspoon to 1 tablespoon chopped fresh
    jalapeño pepper
1 teaspoon tandoori spice blend
1 bag (1 pound) frozen leaf spinach,
    thawed
Salt and freshly ground black pepper

1. In a large skillet over medium heat, heat oil. Add onion, jalapeño, and spice blend and cook, stirring, until onion is soft, about 4 minutes.

2. Add spinach and cook, stirring, until liquid is evaporated, about 5 minutes. Season to taste with salt and pepper and serve.

Collard Greens with Ham

Serve this Southern classic on New Year's Day—eating greens is meant to bring wealth in the coming year.

PREP TIME: 5 MINUTES • COOK TIME: 15 MINUTES • MAKES: 4 TO 6 SERVINGS

½ cup frozen chopped onion

2 tablespoons butter

2 ounces baked or boiled ham, chopped
   (½ cup)

2 boxes (10 ounces) frozen chopped
   collard greens, thawed and drained well

Salt and freshly ground pepper

1 to 2 tablespoons cider vinegar

1. In a nonstick skillet over medium heat, melt butter. Add onion and cook, stirring occasionally, until golden, about 4 minutes. Add ham and cook until beginning to crisp, 2 to 3 minutes.

2. Add greens and cook, stirring, until tender, about 4 minutes. Season with salt and pepper. Just before serving, stir in vinegar.

Spinach and Squash Gratin

This make-ahead side is a great vegetable dish for a buffet or to bring to a potluck.

PREP TIME: 5 MINUTES • COOK TIME: 40 MINUTES • MAKES: 6 SERVINGS

1 tablespoon butter
½ cup frozen chopped onion
1 bag (1 pound) frozen leaf spinach, thawed and squeezed to remove excess moisture
1 cup heavy cream
4 ounces cream cheese
½ teaspoon seasoned salt
2 cups frozen diced butternut squash
¼ cup grated Parmesan cheese
Salt and freshly ground black pepper

1. In a nonstick medium skillet over medium heat, melt butter. Add onion and cook until softened, about 4 minutes. Add spinach, cream, cream cheese, and seasoned salt. Cook, stirring occasionally, until cream cheese is smooth.

2. Stir in squash and 2 tablespoons Parmesan. Season with salt and pepper. Transfer to a greased 9-inch pie pan. Sprinkle remaining Parmesan on top. (Can be made 1 day ahead, covered and refrigerated.)

3. Bake in a 400°F oven until bubbling and golden on top, about 30 minutes.

VARIATION

Spinach and Squash Crêpes
Spoon ½ cup filling onto each of 8 ready-made crêpes (found in the refrigerated section), roll up and place in a greased 13 x 9-inch baking dish. Sprinkle shredded Swiss cheese on top and bake until cheese is melted and crêpes are hot, about 20 minutes.

Sautéed Butternut Squash with Ginger Butter

This rich dish pairs very well with roast pork, turkey, or chicken.

PREP TIME: 5 MINUTES • COOK TIME: 5 MINUTES • MAKES: 6 SERVINGS

4 tablespoons butter
1 bag (1 pound) frozen diced butternut
 squash
2 tablespoons jarred candied ginger purée
Salt and freshly ground black pepper

1. In a nonstick 12-inch skillet over medium-high heat, melt butter. Add squash and cook until tender and golden on the edges, 4 to 5 minutes.

2. Add ginger purée and stir until combined. Season to taste with salt and pepper and serve.

Ratatouille

This slow-cooking mixed vegetable dish melts in your mouth and pairs nicely with Herbed Marinated Lamb Chops (p. 38). Don't bother peeling the eggplant.

PREP TIME: 20 MINUTES • COOK TIME: 45 MINUTES • MAKES: 6 TO 8 SERVINGS

2 medium eggplants (8 to 10 ounces each), cut into ½-inch dice
Salt and freshly ground black pepper
3 tablespoons extra-virgin olive oil
2 teaspoons jarred minced garlic
1 bag (1 pound) frozen sliced zucchini
2 cups frozen pepper stir-fry blend (with onions)
1 can (28 ounces) crushed tomatoes in purée

1. Place eggplant in a colander and sprinkle with 1 teaspoon salt. Toss to coat. Let stand in sink for 15 minutes. Rinse eggplant and pat dry with paper towels.

2. In a nonstick 12-inch skillet over medium-high heat, heat 2 tablespoons oil. Add eggplant and cook, stirring, until soft and browned, about 7 minutes. Transfer to a plate.

3. Add remaining tablespoon of oil and garlic to pan and cook, stirring, over medium heat until golden, 2 minutes. Return eggplant to pan, add zucchini, peppers, and onions and cook, stirring occasionally, 4 minutes. Add tomatoes and simmer, partially covered, until vegetables are very tender and sauce is thick, 30 to 35 minutes. Season to taste with salt and pepper.

VARIATION

Ratatouille Crêpes with Hollandaise Sauce
Prepare the ratatouille as directed above. Prepare hollandaise sauce according to package directions. Warm 8 crêpes according to package directions, then spoon ½ cup filling onto each. Roll up. Place 2 crêpes on each plate and spoon hollandaise sauce over.

Chili Corn

Add more red pepper if you like a spicier dish. Serve this with Tostadas de Puerco (p. 67).

PREP TIME: 5 MINUTES • **COOK TIME: 10 MINUTES** • **MAKES: 4 SERVINGS**

2 tablespoons butter
2 teaspoons chili powder
2 teaspoons jarred minced garlic
2 boxes (10 ounces each) frozen white or
   yellow corn
3 scallions, thinly sliced
⅛ teaspoon red pepper flakes
Salt and freshly ground black pepper

1. In a medium saucepan over medium heat, melt butter. Add chili powder and garlic and cook, stirring, until garlic is golden, 2 to 3 minutes.

2. Add corn and cook, stirring occasionally, until tender, about 5 minutes. Stir in scallions and pepper flakes and season with salt and black pepper to taste.

Jeff's Favorite Creamed Corn

Serve with Fried Chicken with Cream Gravy (p. 5) for a gloriously decadent meal.

PREP TIME: 5 MINUTES • COOK TIME: 7 MINUTES • MAKES: 4 TO 6 SERVINGS

1 cup heavy cream
2 boxes (10 ounces each) frozen white
   corn, thawed
2 scallions, thinly sliced
Salt and freshly ground black pepper

1. Combine cream and corn in a medium skillet and bring to a boil. Reduce heat and simmer, stirring occasionally, until thickened, about 5 minutes.

2. Add scallions and simmer 2 minutes more to develop flavor. Season with salt and pepper.

Sautéed Peas with Lemon

These brightly flavored peas would go well with sautéed white-fleshed fish, like Dover sole or halibut.

PREP TIME: 5 MINUTES • COOK TIME: 10 MINUTES • MAKES: 4 SERVINGS

⅓ cup frozen chopped onion
¼ teaspoon dried thyme
1 tablespoon butter
1 box (10 ounces) frozen baby peas
1 teaspoon finely grated lemon zest

1. Cook onion and thyme in butter in a small skillet over medium heat, stirring, until golden, about 3 minutes.

2. Add peas, lemon zest, and 2 tablespoons water to skillet and cook over medium heat, stirring, until peas and onions are tender, about 4 minutes. Season to taste and transfer to a bowl.

VARIATION

Sautéed Asparagus Tips with Lemon
Substitute 1 box (10 ounces) frozen asparagus tips for the peas. Prepare as directed above.

Soy-Roasted Green Beans

The strong flavor of soy and a subtle touch of ginger really complement the sweetness of the beans. Serve these alongside any roasted meat or poultry.

PREP TIME: 5 MINUTES • COOK TIME: 18 MINUTES • MAKES: 4 TO 6 SERVINGS

¼ cup sliced almonds, for garnish
1 pound fresh green beans, trimmed
1 tablespoon vegetable oil
2 teaspoons minced garlic
3 tablespoons soy sauce
¼ teaspoon ground ginger

1. Place rack in upper third of oven and heat oven to 500°F. Line a baking sheet with foil.

2. Spread almonds in an even layer on prepared pan and place in oven until toasted, 2 to 3 minutes. Transfer to a bowl and set aside.

3. Rinse green beans, but do not pat dry. Transfer beans to the same pan. In a small bowl, whisk together oil, garlic, soy sauce, and ginger. Drizzle mixture over beans, toss until coated, and arrange beans in an even layer.

4. Roast in oven until tender and beginning to brown, 10 to 15 minutes. Transfer to a bowl. Sprinkle almonds on top and serve immediately.

Portobello and Green Bean Casserole

You can assemble this casserole up to 2 days ahead and store it, covered, in the refrigerator. Just bake 5 to 10 minutes longer. This is a perfect side dish for Thanksgiving.

PREP TIME: 15 MINUTES • BAKE TIME: 30 MINUTES • MAKES: 4 SERVINGS

3 tablespoons butter

2 packages (6 ounces each) sliced fresh portobello mushrooms

1 cup frozen chopped onion

¾ cup heavy cream

¾ cup low-sodium chicken broth

1 box (10 ounces) frozen cut green beans, thawed

Salt and freshly ground pepper

2 tablespoons grated Parmesan cheese

1. Heat oven to 400°F. Butter a 1½-quart shallow casserole dish. In a 12-inch nonstick skillet over medium heat, melt butter. Add mushrooms and cook, stirring, 3 minutes. Add onion and cook, stirring, 4 minutes more, until mushrooms are tender.

2. Add cream and broth and bring to boiling. Reduce heat to medium-low and simmer until liquid is reduced by half, about 5 minutes longer. Stir in green beans and season to taste with salt and pepper. Transfer to prepared dish. Sprinkle cheese on top.

3. Bake in top third of oven until bubbly and cheese is golden, 25 to 30 minutes. Let stand 5 minutes before serving.

Golden Potato Salad with Green Chilies

Sour cream adds moisture and tang to this potato salad. Serve warm or at room temperature with meat, poultry, or fish.

PREP TIME: 10 MINUTES • COOK TIME: 20 MINUTES • MAKES: 6 SERVINGS

2 pounds Yukon gold potatoes, peeled and
   cut into 1-inch chunks
¾ cup low-fat sour cream
1 can (4.25 ounces) chopped mild green
   chilies
½ tablespoon apple cider vinegar
Salt and freshly ground black pepper
3 tablespoons chopped cilantro (optional)

1. Place the potatoes in a large saucepan with cold water to cover. Bring to boiling over high heat. Reduce heat to medium and simmer until tender, about 15 minutes. Drain in a colander and let cool 5 minutes.

2. In a large bowl, whisk together sour cream, chilies, vinegar, 1¼ teaspoons salt, and ¼ teaspoon pepper. Add potatoes and toss well. Just before serving, add the cilantro and toss.

Baked Sweet Potatoes with Maple-Chipotle Butter

If you have time you can bake the potatoes the old-fashioned way—on a baking sheet in a 400°F oven for about 50 minutes. I like them with Perfect Roast Chicken (p. 87).

PREP TIME: 5 MINUTES • COOK TIME: 12 MINUTES • MAKES: 4 SERVINGS

4 medium sweet potatoes or yams (about 6 ounces each), scrubbed
4 tablespoons (½ stick) butter, softened
1 ½ tablespoons pure maple syrup
1 teaspoon canned chipotle chiles in adobo, finely chopped
Salt

1. Using a fork, pierce potatoes a few times, place together in microwave and cook at full power until fork tender, 10 to 12 minutes.

2. While potatoes are cooking, stir butter, maple syrup, and chipotles with a fork until blended. Season with salt.

3. Split sweet potatoes and spoon 1 table-spoon of the maple butter into each. Serve immediately, with remaining maple butter on the side.

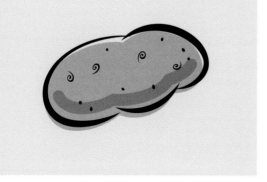

Creamy Dreamy Mashed Potatoes

To make these potatoes ahead, prepare as directed, then transfer to a greased 1-quart casserole or ovenproof bowl and refrigerate up to 2 hours. Bake in a 350°F oven until hot and golden, about 20 minutes.

PREP TIME: 5 MINUTES • COOK TIME: 15 MINUTES • MAKES: 4 TO 6 SERVINGS

1 bag (24 ounces) diced potatoes (hash brown or golden)
2 tablespoons butter
¼ teaspoon salt
¼ teaspoon freshly ground black pepper
½ cup heavy cream

1. Place potatoes in a medium saucepan with cold water to cover. Bring to boiling over medium-high heat. Reduce heat to medium and simmer until potatoes are tender, about 10 minutes. Drain and return to saucepan.

2. Mash potatoes with a masher until finely crumbled. Add butter and ¼ teaspoon each salt and pepper. Add cream gradually, beating with a wooden spoon until fluffy and smooth. Season to taste with additional salt and pepper, if desired.

VARIATION

Lumpy Garlic Smashed Potatoes
Add 4 peeled and lightly crushed garlic cloves to water before cooking potatoes. Cook potatoes as directed above, but do not mash them. Beat in cream and season to taste with salt and pepper.

Juana's Cheesy Fried Spuds

These are great served with bottled ranch dressing for dipping. Serve them with Oven-Fried Buffalo Wings (p. 20) for a fun (and filling!) weekend meal.

PREP TIME: 5 MINUTES • COOK TIME: 20 MINUTES • MAKES: 4 SERVINGS

¼ cup extra-virgin olive oil
1 bag (1 pound) blanched diced hash browns
1 cup shredded cheddar cheese
Salt and freshly ground black pepper

1. Heat oil in a heavy medium skillet over medium-high heat. Add potatoes and cook, turning occasionally, until browned on the outside and tender inside, 15 to 20 minutes.

2. Remove potatoes from heat; sprinkle with cheese. Season lightly with salt and pepper and serve.

Zippy Oven Fries

You can serve these fries as a main dish topped with shredded Cheddar and Quick 'n' Spicy Beefy Chili (p. 63).

PREP TIME: 5 MINUTES • COOK TIME: 35 MINUTES • MAKES: 4 SERVINGS

Vegetable oil cooking spray
1 bag (1 pound) wedge-style oven fries
1 teaspoon Cajun seasoning blend
⅓ cup mayonnaise
2 teaspoons fresh lemon juice
Salt and freshly ground black pepper

1. Heat the oven to 450°F. Line a baking sheet with foil and spray with vegetable oil cooking spray.

2. Place potatoes on prepared pan, sprinkle with seasoning, and toss to mix. Arrange potatoes in an even layer. Bake until edges are beginning to brown, 25 to 30 minutes.

3. Meanwhile, in a small serving bowl, stir together mayonnaise and lemon juice. Season the fries with salt and pepper and serve hot with the mayonnaise mixture on the side.

Gingered Potatoes

These spicy potatoes marry well with plain grilled or roasted meats, poultry, and fish.

PREP TIME: 5 MINUTES • COOK TIME: 15 MINUTES • MAKES: 4 SERVINGS

2 tablespoons jarred chopped ginger or 1
   (2- x 1-inch) piece peeled fresh ginger
3 garlic cloves, peeled, or 1 tablespoon
   jarred minced garlic
½ teaspoon turmeric
¼ cup vegetable oil
1 bag (24 ounces) blanched diced
   potatoes
½ teaspoon salt
½ teaspoon freshly ground black pepper

1. In the bowl of a food processor with the steel blade attached, combine ginger, garlic, turmeric, salt, and pepper. Process until a paste forms.

2. In a nonstick 12-inch skillet over medium heat, heat oil. Add ginger mixture and stir 1 minute. Add potatoes and cook, stirring occasionally, until potatoes are crispy outside and tender inside, 10 to 14 minutes. Serve hot.

Quick Potato Gratin

You can easily double this recipe for 8 servings. Prepare step 2 in a large saucepan, then transfer potato mixture to two 9-inch pie pans or 8-inch-square glass baking dishes.

PREP TIME: 10 MINUTES • **BAKE TIME: 35 MINUTES** • **MAKES: 4 SERVINGS**

1 tablespoon unsalted butter
⅔ cup frozen chopped onion
1 cup half-and-half
1 bag (1 pound) frozen shredded hash browns
½ cup (2 ounces) shredded Gruyère or other Swiss cheese
½ teaspoon salt
¼ teaspoon freshly ground black pepper

1. Heat oven to 400°F. Butter a 9-inch pie pan or 8-inch square glass baking dish.

2. In a medium saucepan over medium heat, melt butter. Add onion and cook, stirring, until softened and golden, about 4 minutes. Add half-and-half and potatoes and cook, stirring, until potatoes are thawed. Stir in cheese, salt, and pepper.

3. Transfer potatoes to prepared baking dish and bake in the middle of the oven until potatoes are tender inside and golden on top, about 35 minutes. Remove from oven, let cool 10 minutes, then serve.

1-2-3 House Salad

You may never want to buy bottled dressing again. This almost-instant recipe makes enough vinaigrette to dress 3 to 4 salads; keep it in a covered jar in the refrigerator for up to 2 weeks.

PREP TIME: 5 MINUTES • MAKES: 1 CUP DRESSING

¾ cup extra-virgin olive oil
¼ cup red wine vinegar
1 tablespoon Dijon mustard
½ teaspoon salt
¼ teaspoon freshly ground black pepper
1 bag (10 ounces) salad greens

1. Combine oil, vinegar, mustard, salt, and pepper in a glass jar. Cover with lid and shake well to blend.

2. Place salad greens in a large bowl. Add 3 to 4 tablespoons dressing and toss well. (Add more or less dressing as desired.)

VARIATIONS

Add fresh herbs in season to the lettuce before mixing in the vinaigrette.

Substitute a flavored mustard (such as tarragon or curry) to the dressing.

Cool Cucumbers in Yogurt

Serve this refreshing Indian-inspired side dish with spicy meats and fish.

PREP TIME: 10 MINUTES • MAKES: 4 SERVINGS

½ teaspoon ground cumin
1 cup plain yogurt, preferably whole-milk
Pinch cayenne pepper
Salt and freshly ground black pepper
1 European cucumber (12 ounces), peeled

1. In a small dry skillet over medium heat, toast cumin, stirring, until fragrant, about 2 minutes. Transfer to a medium bowl. Stir in yogurt, cayenne, and ¾ teaspoon salt.

2. Cut cucumber in half lengthwise. Using a the end of a teaspoon or a melon baller, scoop out seeds. Thinly slice cucumber crosswise. Add to yogurt mixture and stir well. Season to taste.

Seedy Slaw

This creamy slaw is perfect to take to a potluck: coleslaw improves as it sits, so it's best to make this dish ahead of time.

PREP TIME: 5 MINUTES • COOK TIME: 2 MINUTES • MAKES: 6 TO 8 SERVINGS

2 teaspoons mustard seeds
½ cup mayonnaise
3 tablespoons white vinegar
1 bag (1 pound) shredded cabbage
Salt and freshly ground black pepper

1. In a small dry skillet over medium heat, toast mustard seeds, shaking pan, until seeds begin to pop. Remove from heat and transfer to a large bowl. Add mayonnaise and vinegar and whisk until blended.

2. Add cabbage and toss well. Season with salt and pepper.

Herbed Tomato Salad

Tiny sweet tomatoes are available in the supermarket year round, so this salad is quick to whip up any time of year.

PREP TIME: 10 MINUTES • MAKES: 8 SERVINGS

1 pint grape tomatoes, halved
1 pint yellow pear tomatoes, halved
2 tablespoons extra-virgin olive oil
1 tablespoon chopped fresh mint or
   parsley
2 teaspoons balsamic vinegar
Salt and freshly ground black pepper

In a bowl, combine tomatoes, oil, mint, and vinegar. Toss until combined. Season to taste with salt and pepper.

Creamy Cheese Polenta

Warming and delicious, this cool-weather favorite is a perfect side for grilled or roasted meats, like Herbed Marinated Lamb Chops (p. 38) or Easiest Beef and Vegetable Stew (p. 30).

PREP TIME: 5 MINUTES • COOK TIME: 10 MINUTES • MAKES: 4 SERVINGS

½ cup instant polenta
Salt
⅓ cup heavy cream
½ cup shredded Monterey Jack cheese
Freshly ground black pepper

1. In a heavy medium saucepan over medium-high heat, combine polenta, 2 cups cold water, and ½ teaspoon salt and bring to boiling, whisking constantly.

2. Reduce heat to medium-low and simmer, whisking often, until mixture is thickened, about 5 minutes. Add cream and cheese and whisk until warm and creamy. Season with salt and pepper to taste and serve.

VARIATION

Substitute your favorite semi-soft cheese, such as Swiss, fontina, or Gorgonzola for the Monterey Jack. Prepare as directed above.

Cranberry-Orange Skillet Stuffing

This tasty stuffing combines classic Thanksgiving dishes in one sweet and savory side.

PREP TIME: 5 MINUTES • COOK TIME: 10 MINUTES • MAKES: 4 TO 6 SERVINGS

⅓ cup dried cranberries
2 tablespoons unsalted butter
1 teaspoon finely grated orange zest
1 box (6 ounces) low-sodium stuffing mix
Salt and freshly ground black pepper

1. In a medium saucepan over high heat, combine cranberries and 1½ cups water. Bring to boiling.

2. Stir in butter and orange zest, then stir in stuffing mix. Cover and remove from the heat. Let stand 5 minutes. Fluff with a fork and serve.

VARIATION

Apple-Walnut Stuffing
Omit orange peel and cranberries. Substitute 1 small apple, diced, and ⅓ cup chopped walnuts. Prepare as directed above.

Nutty-Herbed Rice Pilaf

The technique of cooking rice briefly in oil or butter before simmering in a flavorful liquid results in a dish known as a pilaf. If you prefer, omit the peas. Couscous can also be prepared using this method; just use 1 cup couscous and shorten the cooking time to 5 to 7 minutes.

PREP TIME: 5 MINUTES • COOK TIME: 30 MINUTES • MAKES: 4 SERVINGS

½ cup pecans
1 cup frozen chopped onion
2 tablespoons unsalted butter or olive oil
1½ cups long-grain white rice
1 can (14 ounces) low-sodium chicken broth
½ teaspoon dried thyme
Salt and freshly ground black pepper
1 cup frozen green peas, thawed

1. Roast nuts in a heavy medium saucepan over medium heat, stirring, until toasted, about 4 minutes. Let cool, then chop.

2. Cook onion in butter in same saucepan over medium heat, stirring, until softened, about 5 minutes. Add rice and stir 1 minute.

3. Stir in broth, 2 cups water, thyme, ½ teaspoon salt and ¼ teaspoon pepper. Bring to a boil, reduce heat to low, cover and cook until rice is tender, 15 to 20 minutes.

4. Stir in peas and nuts, cover, and let stand 5 minutes.

VARIATIONS

Fruited Pilaf
Omit peas. Substitute 1 cup raisins.

Main-Dish Rice Pilaf
Stir 3 cups chopped roasted vegetables or cooked beef, chicken, or seafood into the finished rice.

Cinnamon Cornbread

Cinnamon adds another dimension to this Southern classic. Serve it with Glazed Ham with Pineapple and Onions (p. 95).

PREP TIME: 5 MINUTES • BAKE TIME: 15 MINUTES • MAKES: 6 TO 8 SERVINGS

6 tablespoons unsalted butter
1 ½ cups self-rising cornmeal mix
1 cup all-purpose flour
⅓ cup sugar
½ teaspoon ground cinnamon
2 large eggs, lightly beaten
1 cup milk

1. Heat oven to 450°F. In an 8- or 9-inch cast-iron skillet, melt butter. Tilt pan to coat the bottom, then pour butter into a heatproof measuring cup.

2. In a medium bowl, stir together cornmeal mix, flour, sugar, and cinnamon. Add eggs and milk. Stir until just blended, then stir in butter.

3. Using a rubber spatula, scrape the batter into the skillet and smooth the top. Bake until golden and springy to the touch in the center, about 15 minutes. Let cool in pan 10 minutes before serving.

VARIATION

Spicy Cornbread
Reduce sugar to 3 tablespoons and substitute ½ teaspoon crushed red pepper flakes for the cinnamon. Prepare as directed above.

Quick 'n' Easy Parmesan Muffins

These savory muffins pair nicely with Top Round Beef Roasted Over Vegetables (p. 91).

PREP TIME: 5 MINUTES • BAKE TIME: 20 MINUTES • MAKES: 9 MUFFINS

Vegetable oil cooking spray
1 cup self-rising cake flour
2 tablespoons grated Parmesan cheese
1 tablespoon sugar
½ cup sour cream
1 large egg, lightly beaten

1. Heat oven to 400°F. Spray 9 cups of a 12-cup muffin pan with cooking spray.

2. In a medium bowl, combine flour, Parmesan, and sugar and whisk until just blended. Add sour cream and egg and stir until just combined.

3. Spoon batter into prepared pan and bake until springy to the touch, 18 to 20 minutes. Let cool 10 minutes before serving.

INDEX